Pearls of Wisdom
Communications received inspirationally

Pearls of Wisdom is a series of teachings which will appeal to all, to those simply seeking answers to life's questions and to serious students already on the path of learning.

It is written in a clear, enjoyable style and truly contains many pearls of wisdom, covering the great questions asked by all who seek explanations and enlightenment, giving easily understood answers as well as other topics such as relationships, reincarnation, healing, religion and clairvoyance with truths and observations that are both simple and thought provoking.

The teachings have come from Spirit which accounts for the great feeling of love and gentleness that is felt through them all which time and time again give help and answers but always leave it to the reader to decide for himself, nothing is dogmatic or forced on the reader and the teachings are to enlighten and not to convert. They have been channelled through Doris Forster, a spiritual medium with over twenty years experience of spiritual teaching, clairvoyance and healing both in the UK and overseas.

It is a comforting, helpful collection that will be read and re-read many times, being written in a style that is not only informative but also uplifting and enjoyable.

Brian Allmey

Pearls of Wisdom
Communications received inspirationally

by

Doris L. Forster

Regency Press (London & New York) Ltd.
125 High Holborn, London WC1V 6QA

*With special thanks
to
Elsie Stobbart, Vera Stanniforth,
Mary and Brian Allmey for
their dedicated support,
and to Fred for his enduring patience.*

ISBN 0 7212 0891 6

Printed and bound in Great Britain by
Buckland Press Ltd., Dover, Kent.

There is not room for Death
Nor atom that his might could render void:
Thou – Thou are Being and Breath,
And what Thou art may never be destroyed.

Emily Bronte

I dedicate this book to my father Walter Peters,
without whom it would not have been written.

CONTENTS

PREFACE

This little book was not meant to be a composition of sermons. It is a book which we hope will bring some enlightenment to those who are seekers of the truth, the great reality, the spiritual truth.

We are grateful to those who gave the time and of themselves to make it possible. We acknowledge with thanks and gratitude the love and the selfless desire to be of service that has been made available to us.

It is of no importance to us whether we are acknowledged as part of the great reality, but we are concerned with the lack of true spiritual love amongst mankind. It is our desire to give love and to bring light where there is darkness, to feed the hungry spirit and be instrumental in being part of a united world. When the human spirit has acquired the peace within, then the peace without shall be a possibility. When all the minds of all the academics in this world have learned to understand the knowledge they acquired, and there can be that knowledge with this understanding, then there will be peace.

So, we have tried and we are trying to be instruments of peace, helping and trying to be keepers of the flame, trying to be the key that unlocks a starved and hungry mind, but most of all we are servants of God and it is totally irrelevant what you call your God as long as He is love. We always try to come when we are needed, we are always there. We came with peace and we are leaving you in peace.

Thank you all. May your God be with you.

INTRODUCTION

This volume of inspired teachings of the Spirit has one advantage above all, in comparison with many similar publications; it brings head and heart together for the understanding of everyman.

Frequently spiritual philosophising can be tedious when it is all of pure intellect, and can be off-putting when it is all emotion. Balancing the two, Doris Forster and the influencing minds working through her have produced pages which inspire, comfort and strengthen people in all circumstances. If some do not bother to "take time to smell the roses" along life's way, then they certainly would do well to take time to absorb some of these Pearls of Wisdom which would serve them well in an understanding of themselves and of their place in the universal scheme of all.

Don Galloway

CHAPTER 1

WHY?

We are not here to play, to dream, to drift. We have hard work to do and loads to lift. Shun not the struggle – face It – 'tis God's gift.

Goethe

We have come trying to answer a question which at one point in their life, everybody asks as they survey their life and take stock – what is it all about? Why me? Why do I feel so heavy? Why is this particular lifespan I have chosen so very hard, so difficult? Why has my loved one died – he who has never harmed a soul but was so good, so kind? Why is my loved one suffering? Why is God so silent in my hour of despair? So let us call it WHY, with a big question mark.

When you are a small child sitting at the footstool of your elders you listen with your mind and your brain. The mind is independent of the brain, but links to it and the brain is the one that is first influenced in all you absorb. As you listen you are made aware of God. God is love, God created you, God understands all and you learn your first lesson in laughter, in joy, in sorrow and in pain. Those who love you will punish you, arms that held you in a warm embrace a few minutes earlier, can a few minutes later come down in anger on your physical body. You are confused, bewildered and lost: one minute you are told that love is kind, love is gentle and is forgiveness, the next minute you are in pain and suffering at the hand of that loved one. Confusion, bewilderment and question marks rise in front of your eyes . . . why . . . and your self starts to question. Why is this, why is that, why if God is love is there so much pain. As the older members of your family start their journey back to their spiritual home and you see sorrow, grief and pain, you are told in answer to the question, "where has Grandpa, Grandma gone", they have gone to God. You are told God is love, it is all peace and light in God's presence, and yet you see the sorrow and pain etched in their faces and once again you are confused. Why? It is too contradictory. Is this the God they talk about who is a symbol of love? Does He really take and give, love you and punish you? So, like your elders, like your parents who are in charge of your physical life, you begin to fear God because you begin to realise that where there is love there is hate, punishment, bad conditions. "I am only going to be loved, cuddled, comforted if I do exactly as I am told by the adults and God will punish me, be angry with me if I don't. He will not love me." So, this small naughtiness and the misbehaviour of childhood can get out of all proportion because of fear replacing love and trust. The confusion grows. We go to church, we attend places of worship because we want to please God and we want to please those who are in charge of our life. We realise now that if we do things that please others we will be praised and we will be loved. If we don't, we have a solitary existence and we are in despair and pain. Very early on in the early years of our physical life, we learn love and fear as they are synonymous, side by side.

Oh, how we long for this unconditional life, just to be told that there is love regardless of what we do or are. We never mean to misbehave or to be destructive. We start the day with full intention to be pleasant, good, bright and truthful, but we are sidetracked, we are influenced by other negative influences and the anguish of having done wrong is enhanced by the fear that we have displeased God and those we love.

Oh, a wise parent teaches unconditional love. A wise parent guides and directs and is there, trying to be love at all times. The mother and father who want a child that is growing up without a disturbed psyche, must love the child and gently show the way to encourage that which is there in abundance in the child, recognise the gifts, bless and embrace them. They talk of a God that is love without condition, a love that is there at all times, but as we are all victims of our environment and products of different cultures, we do not always choose an environment that is very conducive to a quick spiritual growth. In the majority of cases it is a very difficult life condition where we are surrounded by ugliness, physical and material squalor, an existence of poverty, parents who are bitter and frustrated whose hopes are directed towards their offspring so that their hopes can be fulfilled through them as their own have not come to fruition.

God is always within and around us, but, alas, we ignore this fact.

When all is against you, when nothing you try to achieve comes right, it is then you can give thanks for the bounty of God and see the God in all things living and you will succeed because the love and the light of God that you cling and adhere to will guide you onto a path of light and beauty. No man can destroy the spirit of life. They can mutilate, kill and end your physical, but cannot destroy your spiritual and when you realise that you are invincible, you are walking in the light and love of God.

Now before you entered this particular life, you have looked at your spiritual bank balance, have looked at what you have learned and you recognise the shortcomings in your spiritual make-up. Because you are restless and refreshed as you have been in your spiritual retreat – in your home – you look around and you realise the personalities you have to meet in order to overcome your shortcomings and to learn your lessons. There are debts to be paid back, people who have lifted you up, helped you, guided you without gratitude or reward in their minds, and you decide which type of environment and in which culture are the personalities who can help you an your path of spiritual lessons, then you embark on your journey.

You might have decided just to have a brief touch with a physical vibration and come through a mother who might never hold you in her arms. Your touch is brief with a speedy return to your spiritual home and you reach your spiritual maturity within your spiritual home. You have done a noble thing, for the mother who never held you has wanted to learn the lessons of how to come to terms with the grief of never holding a child in her arms, for she in turn, in a previous life, might not have come to terms with motherhood, abandoned her children or aborted them, and has chosen to go through this life to have a longing for children, only to find that this longing can never be fulfilled. But she can grow with that, for with that lesson she grows stronger and better and will appreciate the privilege of being an instrument to give life.

All your experiences are there for a purpose. A mother who has lost her only child on the threshold of manhood or womanhood, who was looking forward to holding her children's children in her arms so that through the autumn and winter of her life she would have contentment through her grand-children, to see the fruit of her womb prosper and be content, only to have her hopes, her dreams quashed by an act that appears to be cruel and destructive. Her arms are achingly empty, the house hollow and quiet and the meaning to her life is withdrawn. Just the question "Why?" remains, for the child that has left her bereft was good, kind, helpful. Why? These were her lessons, helped by the presence of goodness and awareness. The lesson she had chosen now starts – to accept that the child has gone where it truly belongs, that all that comes through us is just the physical, that it is a privilege to give life, but that we cannot possess another life. Nurture it, love it and let it go, for the letting go is one of the hardest lessons we can learn.

It is at times like that when we have to let go that our true spiritual strength will come to the surface and it will become recognised then that the truth, the only truth is that God is love and the only permanency is the spiritual life. That cruel parting which we think fate has dealt us is only a passing experience, but that love we felt would be there for eternity. We can draw strength from this truth and grow strong. In our moments of weakness – which are necessary for our learning process – some enlightenment will appear and our most sad experiences give us a chance to rise above and be aware of the tears and anguish in others. So we can, when we want to, share in all experiences of life and we all can be noble servants of God by these shared experiences.

You see, God *is* a wise parent. He lets go, He does not judge for He is love. In His arms, the arms of His love, we are free. So, when you are bereft, when you are hurting, when the pain overwhelms you, when the darkness is unbearable, remember your parent is there, with love, for it is in the darkness that you see the stars. It is in the night you learn the lessons of light. Ask your questions. The enquiring mind is a mind that is alive and aware. Fight all that overshadows you and tries to dominate you. God is not domineering, He is free and so are you. Free to love, free to give what has been given to you and most important of all, you are free to live according to God's love.

May the peace of the Great Spirit overshadow you with light.

CHAPTER 2

RELIGIONS

*To man in his fragile craft a rudder has been given
expressly that he may follow the guidance of his insight
and not the caprice of the waves.*

Goethe

In answer to the question – is religion necessary – yes, it is for some people. It is necessary if the individual feels that they are in need of it and, if it helps them in a constructive and positive way, then it is right for them, but many people, once they belong to a religious order or certain creed, are quite overwhelmed by it and they develop a tunnel vision. They are unaware that the great truth runs through all beliefs, that many ways "lead to Rome" – in this case to our Father God – and that each must find their own way to reach their goal. Religion is only harmful when it oppresses a person or retards the spiritual progress. Of course, in many cases where the spiritual progress is retarded or held back, the physical can suffer because of it. Any religion that calms and soothes a troubled spirit will be beneficial for spiritual growth.

Many people have turned away from religion due to the fact of history reminding us that in the name of religion and the name of the Father God, many atrocities have been committed. Man has destroyed, killed and maimed in order to suppress another's belief. No wonder people are turning away from the more orthodox doctrines and are now searching for something comprehensive which envelopes all that contains the breath of God. A new kind of philosophy is breaking through into this world where people are embracing all that is uplifting and frees the human spirit from the shackles of orthodoxy. There are still, and always will be those who need the discipline, the ritual, that a more orthodox religion can give them. It can be a mental and spiritual exercise which helps them to maintain a spiritual discipline in order to put a tight rein on their thoughts so that no demonic thought is able to invade their mind, but unfortunately in some cases they might develop a narrow mindedness which makes them blind and deaf to truths of other religions.

Religion is man-made. When man was created with that wonderful gift of eternal life, he was also given the gift of free will. As far as we can think back and as the biblical records show us, man has abused this gift when he incarnated into flesh. The flesh, as we have been made aware of, has been man's downfall. If you want to use the biblical term, the flesh has been 'sinful', but it was not intended to be that way. It was to be a vehicle to learn, to experience and to be the school-house of learning a material life so that eventually one could graduate into a higher existence. In other words that man, through his experiences in the flesh, will have evolved spiritually as well and come once again nearer to his origin, to be home nearer to the Creator, the Father of all life. But, like all things freely given, these gifts get abused, as long as there are spirits in the flesh with the desire to have power over other fellow men, to influence and manipulate them so that they can maintain their control over others.

From the time man started to walk upright some form of worship has existed. Paganism also contains truth of God, for these people worshipped the earth that brought forth the plants, herbs and vegetables that nourished man, the sun which gave it light and warmth and the moon which achieved the balance between night and day. There were those people who worshipped the light and all that was instrumental in bringing forth the light in the natural world around them, and all that is light, as we know, originates from God. So paganism contains a godly truth. The early believers who worshipped the natural images of the world of nature which, too, is of God's creation, were in fact worshipping God without realising it. There were those who worshipped the darker side. It is the same now as it was in the first stages of man's evolution on this planet when there was the light and the darkness. There will always be people who worship all that is light, all that brings forth goodness, harmony and peace. Only that which is for self-grandiosement, for power and control over others is not of God, for in the worship of God we respect and love our fellow man. Those who worship on the darker side are for self and as there will always be a positive and negative, there will always be light and darkness so until man has learned the lessons to balance within himself the negative and the positive, the struggle to gain power over others via certain religions will continue.

Each spirit is part of a divine plan and each spirit will choose what form, shape or part he or she will play on this stage called life. They might choose the path of the Roman Catholic or Anglo-Catholic where they know that the pomp and ritual is necessary for them to have spiritual discipline, or they may choose the more austere Methodism, Calvinism or Lutheranism – it is left entirely to the individual. There is no judgment towards any religion which is uplifting. A religious belief is a free choice and should be treated as such. We have pointed out that religion should not harm the physical or spiritual body, but should enhance, bring contentment, peace and harmony within.

Can we only serve through religion? Is it only possible to serve God through religion? Well we can serve through religious orders if we so wish, but we serve God just by loving all that is God in all life. For as you know, we always see in others what we see in ourselves. All the good and noble attributes we see in our fellow men are of God and if people irritate us and there are certain negative aspects in their spiritual or physical make-up then we are only too cruelly reminded of our own shortcomings, for these things are within us also. It is just as well to be reminded of the fact that we always see the truth in others because it is within us.

Religions are man-made, but some people are inspired because there are people – Avatars and Masters – who have learned their spiritual lessons well. Even though they could remain in a permanent state of bliss if they wish to, as they have risen above all the coarser emotions and mastered the natural law, in many cases they have chosen to be near this Earth, within the reach of humanity in order to serve. These souls, these Masters, have inspired the people of Earth and are very often the origin of inspiration, being instrumental in forming religious beliefs.

Spiritualism came into this world inspired by one of the Masters to balance the new found belief of Christian Science. There were always people available through whom these ideas could be channelled and the people who made themselves available were aware of their calling, as they termed it, and the role they had to play in this particular part as a founder of a new religion or philosophy. When spiritualism was made popular, everything in that particular area depended on "seeing is believing" and most of the phenomena which took place in the first fifty years of that philosophy was of a physical origin. Since then man has evolved and the majority of phenomena is now of a higher frequency and more of a mental mediumship. More people are becoming aware and learning to tune in to the etheric world to receive information and inspiration. This, too, is no accident as everything happens according to a plan. If King Henry VIII had not succumbed to the desires of his flesh, the majority of the people in England would still be following the Catholic belief. Martin Luther had the strong desire to serve God via the ordinary people by making the Bible available to everyone and translating it. With this act he was forced to make a decision which meant breaking away from Catholicism. He felt with humility that the majority of people were not aware of the truth, because the Latin language was only comprehensible to the theological mind and he wanted to make the truth available to all. He made a written proclamation which he then nailed to the door of the Cathedral of Würtenberg and the evangelical Lutherian Church was founded.

We have two different aspects there. One from a spiritual origin, and one that in biblical terms would be succumbing to the 'sins of the flesh', yet each brought forth a new kind of religion. We learn from this that many ways "lead to Rome" and every religion can be used in the best way as the material is available. The weakness of the then King of England was due to his physical desires and the strength of Martin Luther was his compulsion to serve God with honesty and simplicity. Out of the weakness of a ruler sprang the Church of England, yet the tunnel vision developed and all other truths had to be abolished. People were persecuted, killed, maimed and hunted down. The evidence of those dark days is still to be seen in many homes in the British Isles where the impact of the fear and suffering can still be felt.

God created man to be free and it is man's birthright to worship as he wishes and as he desires, but when man abuses another man's free will he then intervenes in the natural law. God does not punish for when he created the universe there was a perfect just law, the natural law. No-one is exempt from the correct working of that law. If a certain religion you have chosen helps you, uplifts you and brings you peace and contentment, then this is right for you, but if it gives you fear or anxiety and also makes you unhappy then obviously it is not right. Your spiritual belief should set you free. God is not meant to be an object of worship that inspires fear but He should be an inspiration for all the splendour that is in this universe. All God ever wanted, and still does, was for his children to give love to one another, to respect life which he created. He gives love to all that has the breath of life and has furnished each spirit with this love. It is a well that never dries up, but man is inclined to forget it.

Written onto the etheric records, never to be wiped out, is evidence of man's inhumanity towards man, for in the name of religion man has killed, maimed destroyed and suppressed in order to manipulate another spirit, a human life, but there will always be those who will strain against the leash, who are overcome by the very strong desire to serve God by loving their fellow man. In that case there will always be a pioneer who will break free of the chains, for he has realised that only by being free, spiritually free, can he worship God. Worship as you wish but should you harm any living creature, then the effect of the natural law will make itself felt eventually. That is not a threat from God, but simply sowing and reaping, cause and effect.

We accept the fact that religion when used correctly can be very effective and be an aid towards spiritual evolution. If it is abused and negative results are obtained it is harmful and is not of God. All that is right is of God and will always be beneficial, but if it is not of a godly source it is harmful. There is only one thing that will always be right and that is God's love, the justice of the natural law, for these facts are reality. God is love, life and light. By worshipping these virtues and being aware of them in all your fellow men, you will obtain great vision which will take the blinkers off the eyes. Listen, observe and see that which is of God and you will then find the light to enhance your life. You will live your life within God's law and peace will be within you. Try to look with compassion at those who are unable to shake off the blinkers of narrow mindedness. Spare a thought of healing and a blessing to those who dwell in darkness or those who are fanatical and try to persecute and manipulate others, for you now know they too, will be in the light one day. Within all God's creatures is a divine spark which will have to make itself felt in time.

Put your blessings on all those who do not yet understand, for their day will come. Already a great awakening has started. A spiritual light is focused on the planet, Earth, and where there is a spiritual light, God's truth can be found.

CHAPTER 3

THE WORLDS OF LOVE

Beloved voices, dearly familiar, so sorely missed,
Whispering closely in my doubting ear.
It cannot be, they are dead, gone far away
Yet the sound of their voices, filled with love, so near.
Despairing, alone and lost, I prayed for a sign from God
above.
"We are here", sweet voices say, "well and alive in
Elysian Fields,
A World of Love."

Doris Forster

As you are entering into this new age when the century is drawing to a close and a new awakening has started within the human spirit, the different worlds that are intertwined are worlds within worlds and are drawing closer to your world, the physical world. It is true that all worlds are one. There are universes within universes, but the concept of the universe is incomprehensible to the human brain. There is the dawning of this new age that attracts inhabitants from other planets closer to your existence and, as it is with all life, there is a variety and a mixture of personalities that are attracted to all. As you are aware, within the spiritual law of attraction like will be attracted to like. It is not like your law where there is the law of attraction of opposites, the positive and the negative. In the spiritual law only like can exist among like. So if you are a being who is filled with love and positive thought you will attract other beings to you with the same tendency and virtues. If you are the kind that is destructive, misguided and negative, you will then draw to you the same. The more optimistic and the more positive your own thoughts, the more you will attract to yourself.

You are encouraged to save your pennies, in your savings banks where they can accumulate so that you have stored material riches for a rainy day and you learn to be thrifty and sparing with your spending in order to have material riches behind you. You are, or should be doing the same with your spiritual riches. Every negative thought and emotion you manage to turn into a constructive positive one is a penny put into your spiritual bank. The rate of interest and the discount is much higher than in your material world. For, as it says in the natural law, everything shall be returned to you seven times seven, whether in the negative or in the positive.

It takes sixty-three muscles in your face to frown, but only thirteen to smile! Why not try a smile that is the lesser effort? It is so wonderful to see the thoughts of love penetrating the veil into the etheric world. It is like a candle that is lit within the darkness of the night. Every time you send out a thought of love you light a candle and you make these worlds of love a brighter, more shining existence. With that candle you have ignited, you attract to you beings that are drawn like moths round a light. So you are really keepers of the flame of love and light. That is what the Creator intended when He created you, to be keepers of the flame in these worlds of love.

We smile, we are bemused when we tune into your ideology, your philosophy, when the thought that there are other planets inhabited by life is preposterous to the human brain or scientifically improbable. Poor loves, this universe is so vast. There are existences of life forms you cannot comprehend with the narrowness of your brain, and your scientists could not explain it away, yet your greatest scientists, healers, philosophers, academics, are from those planets. They came with advanced knowledge far beyond your knowledge at this present time, to enhance your existence. Harry Edwards, the healer, is one of us. The healers, the ones you call the miraculous healers from Brazil, have been born into your world with the ability to perform – from your point of view – miraculous cures. Some of your well known mediums have been born into your world with a more advanced psychic ability, some of your great trance mediums. Some of your medical geniuses – we mention Dr. Fleming – yes, and Professor Hahn who split the atom, but that was sent to you as a source of energy not to destroy.

You see, what is meant to be dominant in all worlds is the power of love and of course as within each life there is a positive and a negative, or as you call it, the good and the bad, it is up to each individual what they want to be ruled by. There is always one thing that gets into the way of the spiritual evolution, and that is the ego, the ego that misinterprets love, that replaces the spiritual love for all life by a narcissistic self-love, so that man or woman are overcome and even thrilled at the prospect of being in love with themselves or the idea of the greater self, but eventually all love will be purified. So that explains the fact that even those who are born into your world in an advanced evolved state do not actually regress but are sidetracked. We understand the pitfalls of the human spirit that is encased in the physical body and we do not condemn because we all went through that stage of evolution where we stumbled and were held back, and it is through these little falls we have in life that we get time in retrospect to take stock, gather up strength, look up and search forward.

There are beings from these other worlds and especially at this particular time at the dawning of the new age, beings from the Pleiades, mentioned in your Old Testament, who circle around this planet. They live around your world to keep an eye on the increasing growth of destruction which destroys all that is positive and beautiful, because, should a holocaust occur now on your planet it would throw the rest of the universe out of balance and upset the universal balance of other planets. So these beings are attracted to those who wish to preserve this planet, those who are trying to diminish the pollution and the poisoning of your world.

We also have the other side of the coin where those who are determined to have personal self enhancement gain power; who feed on that power which gives them a stimulus and feeds their ego and they will attract those beings who think exactly as they do.

Let us start when you are at the beginning of your earthly life when your imagination is fed on fairy stories, and you are made aware in your nursery years of the power and the fight between good and evil. It is the same as the natural law, the positive and the negative, and there is a constant battle that there should be a balance achieved. At this moment in time a lot of effort and a lot of thoughts of love are needed to achieve this balance as those negative destructive elements manage to gain a dominance at times. You know how desperately hard it is at times to achieve a balance within yourself, to overcome negativity and to be optimistic despite all the obstacles on your pathway of life. You are also aware of the feeling of triumph, joy and love when you achieve this, battle within yourself and let the optimism and the positivity of your higher self be the winner.

It is a cliché in your world that love will find a way. It does and it will. It will find a way to be the dominant factor in all worlds. The human spirit, as is all spirit, is indestructible and whether the fact and the doctrine that life and love are eternal is accepted by orthodoxy is of no consequence, for it is the only truth and we do not come within your orbit to preach a particular doctrine. Our only philosophy is the philosophy of love. Love thyself, know thyself as you are. Be firm in the face of adversity and negativity. No-one has the right trying to overshadow with negativity where there is positivity. There is only one divine right and that is to be love. When you find you are being faced by someone or something that threatens to drain you of your positive life force, that is when you have the divine right to say, "Not with me you don't," You are a child of the universe. You have a right to be here. You are love. You are the keeper of the flame and if people who are within your environment are trying to bring you down from your goal and drag you down to their level, you have the right – it is your eternal birthright – to walk and stay in the light. It is part of your birthright to send them love, to clothe them with love in your thoughts, but if they decide to go their way, if they choose to walk into darkness and your light does not penetrate their darkness, then leave them with love. It is painful for you to leave them for you are love. Let them know, "I am here, I am love, I am light, and my light will be in your darkness when you need it. When you walk through the pitch darkness of the night when no star and no candle is lit upon your path, call out, I shall be there."

For it is in the dark of the night that you can see the stars, it is through the darkest night that you find the love you are seeking. When the voice cried out with deepest agony, "My God, why has Thou forsaken me," God answered back, "I am here my son and I always will be. No matter where you are my beloved children, I shall be there. I will be your candle in your darkest night. I will be the blanket of love when you are starved and shivering. I will be your companion when you are imprisoned in your soul. I will help you to kindle the flame of love. I shall never forsake you. It is only in your negativity that you are forsaking me. I am with you, my beloved, now and always and no matter what assails your worlds of love, I am love, and so are you."

Keep the candle lit. Be the keeper of the flame.

CHAPTER 4

THE WORLD OF THOUGHT AND DESIDERATA

The most pleasant things in the world are pleasant thoughts, and the great art in life is to have as many of them as possible.

Bovee

Many great philosophers who wrote about different ideologies, talked about them, preached them and practised them, were the forefathers. Now there is the Marxist creed and the born-again Christian today. How do you react towards the man or woman who stands up and shouts with a far away look in their eyes, "I am a born-again Christian." What do you say to them. Do you say, "Well done brother, well done sister?" Do you congratulate them on their rediscovery or do you sit back in amazement and bewilderment? All these things have been here before and you know it, deep within you. There is only one thing that will really impress you and that is the action of a person who is aware, the person who realises there is a greater reality beyond this materialism, who knows that to be enlightened – and that is exactly what this means to be a Christian – is to do it and to be it. The true Christian, the true enlightened one will never shout, will never have to go from door to door to say "I'm a Christian, I'm a good fellow. I believe in the Christ." They do it quietly, unobtrusively without drawing any attention to themselves for they will live with love for all mankind.

How can we help this sick world, then, with the born-again Christian? Are they utterly useless? Of course not, they have their uses just like anybody else. With their fervour and their enthusiasm they can ignite another flame. They can see somebody who is on the edge of despair and can help by calling out to them, "I am a Christian, look at me. I was lost and now I am found." So we cannot judge them for everything has its place, everything has its niche, just as we are part of it all. To really think about it, to really have that important impact on your life, you must be what you proclaim to be.

That is of the most importance in all things and in all aspects of life whether you are an academic in a university, the local dustman or the window cleaner, shopkeeper, baker, butcher, or whatever. Whatever you have chosen to be in this life, to your own self be true for, after all the searching and all the delving into different realities, that is what it is all about.

On the other side of the coin, we are going to meet people who appear to do so much good, who are involved in charities and who are here, there and everywhere, always mentioned and always talked about in connection with doing good works. Are their thoughts really involved in this work? Do they really mean what they are doing? Are there thoughts of love when they are involved with people who are less fortunate or is it just something they do for appearance sake to impress others or to achieve some temporary fame as a do-gooder, to ease their conscience?

Really it is amazing when we stop and think about it, how important the world of thought is. When we find ourselves in a position where we actually cannot do good, where we would like to give money to the poor and to help in practical matters but are unable to do so, we can still help those unfortunate people by thinking well, by giving them thoughts of love and kindness. In our busy material world we often meet people in whose company we feel comfortable, who make us feel good just by being in their presence. Their words are no indication for it, or their lifestyles, yet for no apparent reason we feel good. Of course there is a reason, there is every cause to feel well. Those people are thinking well. They are thinking love. They genuinely love their fellow-man and everyone they meet receives exactly the same kind of thought. That explains the feelings we get when we step into houses. We can enter wonderfully luxurious homes where everything perhaps we ever dreamed of is there – beautiful furniture and everything in pristine condition – yet we don't feel well, we don't feel comfortable, we don't feel at home. There will be outward signs of generous hospitality, charming polite manners in the hosts and still we don't feel love, only unease. The explanation for this of course is that in their thought world there is no room for love, genuine love for others and so when there is no love in their minds there can be no imprint of love on the etheric world around them. It is that thought world we are first assailed with when we enter into a homestead. If there is love in any home, no matter how humble, how poor or how rich it may be, if their minds are filled with love there will be love.

We don't always bother to put this into practice. Our mind is infiltrated with thoughts that are very often chaotic, full of self, full of a desire for more riches and yet we rarely stop to try to discipline our thoughts. At times, our thoughts for self are stopped when somebody pushes a begging bowl under our nose and we go and look for our coins to put in, feeling we have done something for somebody else. Of course it is a commendable thing to do to give money, but what a wonderful thing it is when a person takes the time to think well. We spend a lot of energy, time and effort to think negatively of another person. In many instances we look very hard to find the bad, the destructive in mankind because it is so obvious and so apparent, always forgetting that the good, the Divine spark is within them all.

We should realise that our passage through this planet, Earth, is only a brief one, it is like a speedy journey through space, it will be over in a flash and we squander our time wasting our energy on useless things, but with the sound of laughter, the thought of love, you ignite the light and brighten up your very existence with these sounds and thoughts. When you are down, try to remember this and how much beloved you are to the Creator, how with your thoughts you can lift yourself up into the highest and the best. Your thoughts help you build your eternal home, brick by brick. With your thought energy there is no limit for you are your own architect of your home of the future.

When people are in despair and cry out, "Oh my God, what shall I do," we would like to say to them, "Think well. Think well of yourself, think well of your fellow men. Rise above all the negativity and destructiveness that is around you. Visualise the light in your darkness and feed that light with your positive thought." We can imagine what you think now, "Easier said than done. I've been thinking well. I thought he was nice, I believed in him and I believed in her, but what did they do? They have let me down." What they really did is let themselves down. You can forgive, you can rise above it with your thought, but they haven't yet faced up to it and that is the most important thing. If we face up to our own responsibilities and realise that we are responsible not only for our actions, but also for our thoughts and the discipline of our mind, we will try to control our thoughts. Then we will realise that the negative thought which penetrates into our mind can change a high to a low and a feeling of joy into one of depression. We will then make the effort to be more positive and optimistic.

So often we find despair and we are waiting patiently on the edge of the etheric for you to change your way of thinking, for you to reach out with your thoughts towards the light. The instant that happens we are there – we who have gone through that veil, walked where you have walked and understand everything you have experienced, who have chosen to be near you, to be a source of strength to you and to remind you of your true heritage, we who are living in that world of thought. How much effort does it take for you to compose a letter to reach another person in your own world? Yet you can reach us with one thought, a thought of love. No stamp required, no writer's cramp, no effort at all, just a thought of love and we shall be with you, the dearly beloved.

Through the media of your radio, television, books and many other things the word love is often mentioned. You can say it without meaning. You hum tunes containing the words of love, not realising how important true love is for all aspects of life. You are told "sow the seeds of love and you will have a harvest of love." This sowing starts in your mind and it can be testing and tiring for you at times when you are weary and have had a frustrating day at your place of work. You started off optimistic, positive and joyful, trying to do your work with love and a positive feeling, only to be thwarted at every moment and no matter how positive you were you find yourself deflated with negativity creeping in. Of course we understand this and we surround you with love, to encourage you. You can do it, even rise above those conditions of anger, frustration, or violence. Even when your life is threatened and fear overshadows you, it is the physical pain that drives out thoughts of goodwill, especially in the case of a loved one, someone very close to you, who has been made to suffer at the hand of another. Try to rise above that too and remember the law of cause and effect. Everything that is done to harm another will be returned seven times seven. It is an awesome thought, but a fact. By all means defend yourself from those that hurt you – you should not suffer pain needlessly, no-one should – but try not to get into a negative thought pattern. Hate – let it only be a moment, but not for ever, because love, a determined love, wipes out these moments of hate, erasing them and then all you leave in the etheric around you are footprints of love and light.

Every abode you inhabit, every room you reside in will have imprints of love where others will want to dwell. When you are in the presence of another person and you start to feel irritable, unwell and uncomfortable, give them love for they are in need of it. Feed their thought world. Let yours be the stronger more overpowering one. Give them a blessing with your love. Love all that has life and the home that awaits you when you have pierced the veil will be a home shining brightly with love and light, then you, too, can encourage others who are left behind with your thoughts.

Send out a thought today, now, a thought of love, remembering how important it is. This world of yours, the material world, is in need of it. Start it now. Give a thought. Make it a thought of love.

DESIDERATA

These words were written by a monk in the 15th Century. They are wonderful and full of timless wisdom.

Go placidly amid the noise and haste and remember what peace there may be in silence. As far as possible, without surrender, be on good terms with all persons. Speak the truth quietly and clearly and listen to others, even the dull and ignorant, they too have their story. Avoid loud and aggressive persons. They are vexations to the spirit. If you compare yourself with others you may become vain and bitter for always there will be greater and lesser persons than yourself. Enjoy your achievements as well as your plans. Keep interested in your career, however humble. It is a real possession in the changing fortunes of time. Exercise caution in your business affairs for the world is full of trickery, but let this not blind you to what virtue there is. Many persons strive for high ideals and everywhere life is full of heroism. Be yourself, especially do not fain affection, neither be cynical about love for in the face of all aridity and disenchantment, it is perennial as the grass. Take kindly the counsel of the years, gracefully surrendering the things of youth. Nurture strength of spirit to cheer you in sudden misfortune, but do not distress yourself with imaginings. Many fears are born of fatigue and loneliness. Beyond a wholesome discipline, be gentle with yourself. You are a child of the universe no less than the trees and the stars. You have a right to be here, and whether or not it is clear

to you, no doubt the universe is unfolding as it should. Therefore be
at peace with God, whatever you conceive Him to be and whatever
your labours and aspirations in the noisy confusion of life, keep
peace with your soul. With all its sham, drudgery and broken
dreams, it is still a beautiful world. Be careful. Strive to be happy.

The philosophy of these words is timeless, for time is irrelevant.
In your material world time is necessary so you can live an orderly
life, which is how it should be and we are grateful for the time you
make available for the spirit, whether you use the greatest gifts God
gave you, of love and compassion or whether you make time to
think orderly thoughts and meditate to recharge your spiritual
battery. When spiritual energy flows freely through you, you will be
well, in harmony with your physical body and your spirit is
functioning freely according to its need.

We forget about this spiritual freedom which is part of our
existence. Only a free spirit which dominates our striving and
material life can remind us what our true function in life is. Now
what about these gifts of the spirit? What should we do with them?
Everyone can use them as they wish or as they feel it is their right to
do so. It is true that we can only learn from experience, but in too
many cases we don't want to remember our experiences or the
lessons we have learned from them for we do not want to dwell on
the negative past, but it would be well if we could remember the
lessons we have already learned. Not only would they be of great
benefit to our own life, but also to the lives of others. Mostly we are
drawn to the people we feel to be experienced if we are in need of
expert advice. We go to medical specialists with experience if
something ails us. We go to people for spiritual counselling who
have the experience to give it. So we too can be experts on how to
live our life constructively by learning to use the spiritual gifts with
which we are endowed for the benefit of all mankind. The choice is
entirely ours.

Of course, we always return to the fact of the free gift of choice.
We are far from being thrilled by the idea for we don't always want
it. We don't always want to accept the responsibility of choice, so in
order to avoid this, we seek out people who we know to be psychic
so that we can be told which direction to take, what decision to
make, or whether this or that particular plan will come to a very
happy conclusion.

In moments of stress and anxiety we are unable to see clearly because once again we have forgotten how to discipline our thoughts or how to think constructively, so confusion is all around us and within us. We then seek advice and guidance. Naturally there are people who have the ability to tune in to the Akashic records in order to see what lies ahead for us. Should we be told if there is disaster ahead, when illness will strike us down or accidents will happen, or even of a premature departure from this physical world? Do you want to know that? Many people might say, "Oh, I would rather know than not know." If all of you knew what lies ahead, if you knew exactly what decisions to make and which way to go, if you had all the wisdom and spiritual maturity to do everything correctly, to do the right thing at the right time with never a moment of discontentment or indecisiveness only assurity in all you do and think – would you be here? No you wouldn't need to be here. You are here to learn these things. You are here to make decisions on your own, to step out into the unknown at times and to do it optimistically and positively, realising that all you do is part of your learning process which is really what it is intended to be.

Unfortunately, life is very confusing, particularly in this century. Mankind has evolved and the mental vibrations are higher and finer than they have ever been. Man has learned to enquire deeper into the mysteries of life and mysticism has become an acceptable trendy subject, yet still we don't appear to receive the answers we are seeking. Despite all of this, we are still groping in the dark, still lost, needing advice and help more than ever. Of course, as long as there are souls that are incarnated in the flesh and wish to learn, there will always be those ready and willing to give advice and counsel and there will be those that are only too eager to accept this counsel and abide by it, or ignore it, just as is their choice. We all have a goal. These goals my be different and may have different values, but we are all striving, so we can take comfort from the fact that we are all going to the same school, the school fees for this particular school being a strong desire for spiritual progression, to be nearer the source, an eagerness and willingness to help others, and to give of ourselves in order to bring comfort and love to others.

All this sounds very simple, yet not very easy to do, for we all falter and stumble. We are often very hasty in giving judgement and forgetting the origin of our existence. In times of stress and confusion there are always people willing to listen and to help and we are all here to learn that our decisions are the tools that will aid us on this pathway of spiritual evolution. There is no need to be afraid for we never walk alone. We can take courage from the love that is within us and the love that is given to us freely and we can make time to meditate on the love and the source of this love. Whatever name we wish to give God, He is within us, that is the important message to all mankind. This message is ageless and will always remain so.

Draw strength from that unlimited source that is available to you. You might be weary at this very moment – perhaps your work conditions or your home environment are weighing you down. Straighten your spirit. Remember the gifts you were given and start using them now. Remember that material conditions can weigh you down, but not chain you for you are free. Remember the material words, "You are a child of the universe and you have a right to be here."

CHAPTER 5

"INTO THE WORLD UNSEEN"

Our birth is but a sleep and a forgetting.
The soul that rises with us, our Life's star,
Hath had elsewhere its setting
And cometh from afar.

Wordsworth

Life after death is the great reality. Only when a loved one has left the material world behind do we start to search and to question this reality.

First of all we have to clarify that there is no death, there is no end, there is just a shedding of the physical body which has ceased to function, for the physical body was the shell that housed the spirit. So, where does the spirit go?

The etheric world or the spirit world that is referred to is all around us and is the world the spirit goes to after what you call death has occurred. It consists of a fine nebulous substance and from this fine material the etheric (or astral) body is composed. The spirit is within his etheric body and even though the etheric body is of a much lighter consistency than the physical, it still has many refining and purification procedures to go through. We all accept the radio, we take it for granted, we listen to it and switch it on and off. It is part of our lives and is a medium which transmits, but how do sounds which come through a radio get into it? They are transmitted via the etheric waves of the world. The etheric matter is a substance which seems nebulous and invisible to the naked eye and sometimes only the initiated and trained psychic can penetrate this etheric world with their psychic powers. They can also see the spirit body vacate the physical. It is attached to the physical body by a silver cord, as mentioned by Paul in your New Testament, much as a baby is attached and fed through the umbilical cord in the mother's womb. At the time of birth the umbilical cord is severed and life in the physical starts. Similarly, when the silver cord is severed, life in the spirit world begins again.

When we first start inhabiting the physical body the silver cord is very loose, so as a baby, our spirit is frequently still in its spirit home in the spirit world. Your world has been mystified by what you call "cot deaths". In many cases the cause is that the silver cord is not yet fully attached and the spirit of the infant detaches itself and remains in its spirit home. In cases like that the spirit of the infant might have changed its mind or it will be allowed to remain in the spiritual state so that the parents can learn a lesson of grief by the baby's departure. A brief touch of the earth vibrations might also be sufficient for the infant to learn the lessons it has come to learn.

As the infant starts to grow physically, the silver cord starts to settle in. Complete settlement varies from infant to infant, but normally the age is between three and four. In some cases it might even be longer, so each individual case is different, but you will find that as the memories go back in life it normally happens when that spirit starts to remember its early impression of this life, and from that moment the cord is firmly established.

When we enter this life in order to learn lessons, to progress, to pay debts, Karmic debts, naturally we come with the memory of previous lives wiped out. Again there are cases of exception where there is a memory, but in the majority of cases, the veil of forgetfulness will wipe this out, which is good because it would not be wise to know why we are here and the lessons we have to learn, for it is by striving, trying to do our best and develop more virtues, spiritual gifts, we really learn the lessons.

At night-time during our sleep state when the brain rests the spirit is active, and it is then that the spirit visits its original home, withdrawing to be replenished or to go on missions because the spirit is eager to serve. It may visit loved ones, to be strengthened in their love and reminded of the only true existence or attend meetings in the spirit world and come back with knowledge in order to take up the gauntlet of life on awakening.

Of course we cannot forget our physical for we are influenced by it all the time. Our brain sends messages to the rest of the physical and in some cases to the spirit. We then have images in our sleep state which the brain sends to our consciousness because there are always some problems within us. These images are the reflection of these problems, images we call dreams. Those dreams can reveal a lot to us; they can help us towards self-knowledge for all the great prophets and philosophers have told us "know thyself", and the dream can, if we let it, show us the way to self-knowledge, helping us to solve our problems. There are methods of how to do this and many books have been written on the subject.

It takes some time and effort to find out more about our origin and more about this etheric world which is a world within the material world. Stop, Think! Your loved one is not up there in the clouds, neither are they below the ground being punished. It may sound distant, but they are only a thought away, yet a world away. Their world, the etheric world, could be in your living room where their abode is far more enhanced for the etheric vibrations are finer, quicker and brighter, and it is with your thoughts that you penetrate that world, the power of your thoughts. It is with the power of their thoughts that the spirit entities penetrate ours.

It is up to each individual what type of power you send. You can send that power of love from God which is eternal or use this power for self, to possess, dominate, overshadow, but that would be only a fleeting experience, for all is to be light in the end. All that is dark and unenlightened, which we call evil, is just knowledge which is misused.

So when your loved ones reassure you that they are walking with you, they really are! Your thought is received the instant it is sent out, just as the word that is spoken through the microphone in one building will, the instant it is spoken, be heard with the same speed through your radio via the etheric waves. You carry a big responsibility once you fully realise the strength and power of your thoughts.

Your spirit when it returns to the etheric world, provided you have lived an average decent life, will return to its maturity when you were mentally and physically at your best. No creams, potions or pills are required, only your thoughts. Think well. Remember your thoughts travel fast.

Live well is the rule of love, God's love, and try to accept there is no death. This is just the schoolhouse of learning, or the stage you call life. You have chosen this part. You have chosen to take part in this play and to be in the presence of your fellow actors. You have written the script and now it is up to you how you play your part. Whatever happens in the meantime, there will be a happy ending.

CHAPTER 6

CLAIRVOYANCE

Hands of invisible spirits touch the strings
Of that mysterious instrument, the soul
And play the prelude of our fate.
We hear the voice prophetic, and are not alone.
Longfellow

We would like to talk about the "seeing-beyond", the clairvoyance, because when you look in your dictionary that is what you will find as a definition, clairvoyance, to see beyond. Too many abject truths have been written about it. It is at times a very simple manifestation. At other times it is revered and the person or persons who are giving the clairvoyance are revered, and yet it is pointed out that it is a gift of God, which all gifts are, and many times these gifts are prostituted, sold. What is the right or wrong of them? It again depends entirely on each individual, but we have always taken the example of the one individual, the one who has agreed to co-operate with us in the writing of this book. Her clairvoyance consciously did not manifest itself until well into her thirties, but there were manifestations of the gift quite early on in childhood without her having any awareness.

When children come into this world, they are still very close to the spiritual source and are thus able to tune in and therefore are able to see, to perceive and to sense things that are not of this material world. Unfortunately as the infant mind develops in many cases it is tainted with orthodox indoctrination and influence, being forced to suppress its spiritual and psychic inclinations because in the majority of cases there are not conducive surroundings. That is no accident It is very easy for a gift like clairvoyance to manifest itself, to prosper and grow in empathetic surroundings with very understanding parents and relatives but to choose an incarnation into a very rigid, orthodox upbringing and for these gifts to manifest themselves, then that is another obstacle and striving is indicated in order to overcome that liability.

As it was in this case, there was one parent, the father figure, who understood without being fully aware why he understood, but the mother figure was very socially inclined, things had to be right. She did not like to encourage anything which appeared to be abnormal or talk about something which was different from everything else that she was used to.

So during all her life as an infant there was this very strong sense which even the coarser emotions could not suppress, a sense of belonging to a religious group. Churches gave comfort. The belief in God, the figure of Jesus and the philosophy of the Christ were very much worshiped and loved. The figure of Jesus was a brother figure and gave great comfort at times of stress, disturbance and violence, which was, of course, the Second World War. Right from the first moment it was a very difficult time for this particular life in the reincarnation that was chosen, not only from that aspect, but also memories from the last previous life which had only ended in the 1920s, were still very strong. They were jumbled up with the present one and the veil of forgetfulness had not been able to close completely on memories of that past life which ended young, in her prime, from what was then an incurable disease known as consumption. So, with memories of that, of the house and the environment very strongly with her she was born to the present one and of course the past and the present life were jumbled up, but on top of this, the gift of clairvoyance and clairaudience meant that at times it was very traumatic.

As we all know, when the consciousness rests the subconscious becomes more dominant during sleep time and strong dreams were influencing this young life, very often causing a lot of confusion and very disturbed emotions. Strangely enough, fear from bombs and war weapons was not so strong, even though there was constant noise, constant raids and fear in the atmosphere. In that case the psyche knew that it would survive the war. The memory was so strong that the war would mean survival, not in this case that the best was yet to come, but the worst was yet to come (that was post-war), and somehow the psyche managed to dominate the consciousness, so in this case it was a good thing because it abolished the fear of destruction during the air raids, even though they had been very fierce at times.

So, we point out that in this case, not only was the psychic gift there through many lifetimes, in many lifetimes it had to lie

36

dormant. In the time of the life as a nun it was very strong but could be channelled because of the physical isolation in the cloister with a strong Mother Superior who understood this child and she learned how to channel the psychic gift into spiritual energy. She thus was able to use her psychic gift in helping others, in meditation, laying on of hands and helping people in times of trouble, seeming to be aware that there was trouble and acting upon it, so it was channelled correctly in this particular way. In *this present* incarnation, not only did she choose the gift that has been with her psyche in many, many lifetimes, she also went where there was the genetic factor involved and, coupled with the genetic inheritance, the psychic gift and her own, it was quite strong. There was always this restlessness of energy and this strange sense of being isolated and lonely which all psychics have.

Now, what is this "seeing-beyond"? What does it entail and how does it operate? We all know about what has, up to now, been regarded as a very insignificant organ, the pituitary gland, which is responsible for the hormone distribution to the physical body – very often referred to as the "third eye". It is placed exactly in the centre of the forehead between the two eyebrows. Scientists have now come to realise that this small insignificant organ actually has a very important function in the human body. Hormones are extracted from it and they are essential in the operation of the using of the psychic gift. That is why in many cases where a psychic gift is concerned, you can obtain an imbalance of the hormones, for instance there being in a male an abundance of female hormones and very often a very strong psychicness bringing forward a strong female energy and thus may have an effeminate effect on the male personality. It can also cause havoc in a female person as it can create a disorder and you will find that very many female psychics have gynaecological trouble, also being prone to great mood swings. Again, if this is pointed out, it can be controlled as all psychic gifts can, with discipline of thoughts.

A psychic, consciously or subconsciously, is like a magnet in the etheric world and not all fragments of personalities or spirit entities are of course evolved or an average, ordinary, decent personality. A lot of them are still very negative and destructive so of course a psychic would not only attract all those that are acceptable, but those who come with destructive thoughts, trying to impinge their thoughts into the mind of a possessor of a psychic gift, hence all the great mood swings and in some cases it can result in mental disorder or mental illness. We would not go as far as to say that all schizophrenic or mental disorders are caused by disturbance of the psyche. In some cases it is due to chemical substances or physical disability. In a lot of cases it is a psyche run riot which is an undisciplined psychic gift and in other cases there is trauma from past lives mingled with the present trauma and a mental disorder and disorientation occurs. So not all the delusion of hearing voices is of a psychic influence. A lot of them are an uncontrolled psychic gift, but others can be of a physical origin.

Should one use one's clairvoyance? Is it absolutely essential? There are no hard and fast rules. It again depends entirely on the individual. In many cases you would say it was pre-ordained. It was that he or she had decided that when they incarnated into the physical they would learn to use the psychic gift correctly, learn to channel and discipline it, using it for the benefit of their fellow-men. Others will have decided not to sell the gift and do it for payment, but just to use it in the service of God. We cannot judge or decry anybody's decision because we all make decisions which we are responsible for so we cannot denounce anybody. If a person has decided to use their gift in a commercial way to earn a living from it, using the gift as a profession, or to use it to tell people things which might not be constructive, but destructive or negative, then they alone will reap because it is all "sowing and reaping". They might in a future life come back to suppress the gift or they come back and channel it entirely in the service of God on a spiritual level. It is entirely up to the person concerned.

In this case there has always been a constant struggle against charging or making any monetary gain from the gift, which is totally repugnant. There is also a residue of memory of that life as a nun in the cloister where the gift was used in the service of God. There were lapses as there are in everyone's life, but in that particular life, it was basically, say 90%, used in the service of God. There was of course a very strong religious influence and the spirituality that was in that life and a residue of that memory there which still strongly influences this present life. There is still a desire that this gift should be used to enhance man's earthly life, to aid it on its spiritual progression rather than to retard it. There is never really a total exhilaration of having done any good when there is a monetary charge attached to it. Again, there is no judgment because it was left to the individual to come to terms so that she will decide for herself which is right and which is wrong. There is no pressure put on by us, neither shall we force or remind her what is her duty. You alone decide how to use your gift. You alone say whether you feel it is your duty to go on a path of psychic development and use the psychic gift, and nobody else.

Very often we are amused when we listen in to your clairvoyant services and we hear our name mentioned . . . a named spirit wants you to sit in a circle, or "spirit *wants* you to do this." We might find out there is a gift that a person is trying to suppress. We might remind them of it. We might point out there is one venue available to them if they wish to do so, but we will *not* coerce them into it, neither will we ever attempt to impinge on their mind and suppress that person's own free will. That is not allowed within the natural law.

So when should the clairvoyance be used? When is it right to see beyond? As you know, seeing-beyond is seeing beyond your present dilemma, seeing beyond the fog in which is a person who is in misery and in depression to help them now. It is always noble to bring light where there is darkness, to give hope where there is despair. That is the answer to that question, and when the clairvoyant is sufficiently developed and has learned to channel the energy of his or her mind, positively and correctly in a very disciplined way, then it is the right thing to do.

Contrary to some beliefs, clairvoyance *can* be 100% correct. The average percentage of 75% is acceptable. There should always be the basic truth. We have to take into account in the case of all clairvoyants that the mind is impinged with material sounds, physical thoughts and worries. Very often there is a case of not well being in the physical body so it is very difficult to obtain a very easily balanced state of mind, to be receptive and to tune into the etheric which helps the seeing-beyond. At other times, the chemicals in the sitter's aura might be again of a lower vibration, there might be too much negativity so the aura and the mental process of the sitter is out of focus and out of balance. The clairvoyant has in that case to channel a vast amount of psychic energy in order to obtain a good result. When there is such an apparent struggle it would be wise on the part of the clairvoyant to be totally frank, explain the conditions and perhaps suggest a different time when conditions would be more conducive for a sitting. That would be a wise thing to do and that applies to all manifestations of clairvoyance, whether you have a public performance or demonstration of your clairvoyant powers, whether you sit in a small circle of friends or whether you sit on a one-to-one basis with another sitter, because the results obtained where such conditions exist are not always very favourable, nor are they always very positive for the clairvoyant's physical health. Clairvoyants have learned to obtain the extra strength and energy where perhaps ordinary people who are not aware of their psychic gift or do not possess a lot of psychic gifts are not able to do. They can rise above adverse conditions to obtain a very high frequency, the thought frequency needed to tune into the clairvoyance and are able to do so to give a good manifestation of their clairvoyant powers.

Should the future be told? Should we be able to pierce the veil and tune into a time of the future. Is all pre-ordained? Is everything the clairvoyant predicts which are of futuristic substances, are they all definite, are they what you call part of your fate?

There are various kinds of manifestation. The clairvoyant who can tune in to see or perceive certain things of the etheric world, may be able to see certain images of the sitter or the recipient of that message. There are some things that will happen regardless, but there are other things where man's action can intervene. Remember, there is free will, that man's free will always comes into everyone's life. You are not puppets where strings are pulled by an invisible puppet master who directs you which way you have to go. It is against the natural law and the person who is interfering with another person's life is reaping destructive Karma for himself as much as the person who lets it happen. Free will has to be respected at all times and we do *not* interfere and tell you which direction you have to go. In your prayers when you pray for guidance, we may show you a way. We may try to inspire you and help to lift you out of your confusion, darkness or depression in order that you may walk into the light and be filled with hope once again. If you ignore our signals it is your choice – so be it – for it is your life. If you listen to the inspiration and follow up the guidance you receive, again it is your choice, but some things are predictable and are what you would call, or what any layman would call, pre-ordained, because there is a behaviour pattern with every person and it is predictable in certain conditions how they will react. They will then end up in the situation and conditions that the clairvoyant has seen.

If, for instance, the clairvoyant sees an accident, he or she might be able to warn the sitter to be careful whilst driving in a vehicle. If a plane crash is brought, try not to go on any plane is good advice, but if the recipient has planned a holiday and to cancel that would mean a certain amount of lost money which would be very important to the recipient who is that way inclined, being more ruled by the materialist way of life, then that person will be in that plane crash.

These are just examples. If a person already has a great fear of flying which has always been conquered, who is only too glad to cancel the holiday, be relieved about it and will avoid going on holiday on an aeroplane, being quite happy about it, only to read in the newspapers that in the particular plane he or she should have gone on their physical life would have ended, then the awareness was listened to, adhered to. One person's physical life has been ended and the other one's life was prolonged, so that the life prolonged meant that he or she had been given a chance to learn more lessons and perhaps become even closer to the great reality of life, the spiritual reality.

You see that in all things, the physical brain waves get in the way of all psychic communications. We have to make allowances for it for you are in the physical body and it is only with practice, that is of disciplining your thoughts, that you will be able to rise above material conditions and tune into the frequency which is required to obtain psychic information.

During all this time, as is happening at this very moment, the medium is aware of a pressure on her forehead because she is tuned into the vibration necessary in order for us to work in conjunction, to pass on the information that is required. She has learned that she has to be disciplined in her thoughts and when physical tiredness is very strong, that she has to rest, yet at all times control her thoughts, because even though there is a protective barrier around her with entities that guard, guide and inspire her, others are still able to get through when the guard has been dropped. Of course the ideal way would be if she did not have to be in a physical environment which is ruled by material and financial matters, but she had chosen to learn the lesson of service in the material. There have been several lifetimes where there was physical comfort, a total absence of material worry and there were spoiled and pampered physical lives. Not all the lives, but there was a nucleus of them and a spiritual restlessness had set in because the spirit had then decided to learn to

41

be humble, to realise that any task, no matter how menial, can be of service and is important, in other words, to attach some spiritual substances to the most menial tasks and there were many in this life. She had chosen many different venues to learn and it was not easy. This is a very proud spirit. So, the lessons are nearly finished for this life. Use can be made of the psychic and spiritual gifts and the opportunities will be given but it is entirely up to her to make that decision when the time comes. We shall not put any pressure on her because every being has the right to choose how they wish to use their gift. As we have pointed out, if any gift is used to harm, then the user of that gift is alone responsible and they will have to incarnate again until they learn to use it correctly. It is not dictated to them, but this realisation will dawn upon them as they progress and evolve spiritually.

So you need not judge or fear for people who do not use their gifts as you think they should. Remember, it is their choice and they have the right to choose. It is always better to use it in the service of God. It is always more positive and constructive to use it for the well being of another person, to give light and truth where there is darkness, to bring hope where there is despair, because that not only adds to the well being of the sitter, but also of the giver of that gift. It also adds to the universal truth because each life that has been used or is being used in the service of God is a light which will contribute towards the universal spiritual truth and peace of all creation.

So all of you, whether you are the possessor of the gift of clairvoyance, of healing, a great musical talent or a gift of using words and stringing them together, remember you carry a great responsibility, but that it is for you to decide whether you want to be part of that responsibility, if you want to be part of the Fatherhood of God and the family of man.

CHAPTER 7

THESE GLAMOROUS POWERS

*To live in the presence of great truths and eternal laws –
that is what keeps a man patient when the world ignores
him, and calm and unspoiled when the world praises him.*
                                                            Balzac

At times it appears to the casual observer that psychic gifts are glamorous powers indeed. Like all the gifts the human spirit possesses, these gifts can be used or abused and how you deal with them is left entirely to you. There is a difference if you possess a musical talent, a talent to paint or to sing. With psychic gifts they can let you believe that you are the possessor of some power which can be used to have dominance over other people, or put you into the position where you are revered and idolised because of this power. If the psychic gifts are purely used to help another person who is confused and distressed, a person who has lost sight of the light, got out of touch with the God Force, a person so desperate that all hope has disappeared from their vision and they are surrounded by darkness, in that case you are serving God.

The question often arises when there is evidence of psychic talent, which everyone possesses but some have it to a greater extent than others, whether there should be payment or monetary gain? Again, if somebody gives a service and the service is given with love and spiritual generosity, with total disregard for self enhancement, there would be no reason why payment for the service should not be given, but as in many cases in your life in the material world, there are psychics who obtain good results and on the basis of this are hungry for more material wealth.

In order to understand these gifts, you have to be aware that when you use the gift it takes some life force and strength away from the physical, so you have to learn when to stop and when not to do it, as in most fields where there are ethical rules, you have to be aware how to use your psychic gift. You will learn this when you have chosen a path of selfless, truthful psychic service and you will then be aware when it is correct or when it is just a figment of your imagination. A psychic has to have imagination because the psychic has to learn to visualise, to raise his or her mental vibrations in order to tune into the etheric world to obtain the information that the sitter wishes to know. We do not judge at all what is right and what is wrong. We are just here to give information to those who wish to receive it. The true seeker will know from within which path to choose in the psychic field.

Perhaps you are sitting in a development circle and your psychic gift is unfolding, you are learning how to tune in, how to use your clairvoyance – in other words your far-seeing ability or seeing-beyond – or clairaudience, your ability to hear beyond this world has made itself apparent and you wish to use these gifts to help people in distress. It is a noble thought but there are many temptations. There will be times when you should not speak, and you will. You have tuned into the etheric world, you are aware of beings around a fellow man and you point them out, so you give what you see, you give what you hear and you speak without discrimination. Then you find that the people who are the receivers of your messages are perturbed and confused if you are unabashed, showing no signs of conscience or thought in the matter because you believe you have seen the truth and you have heard the truth so you are the giver of the truth. It may be so when you are developing your psychic gifts, but with that development comes a great responsibility and in order to be a discerning and sincere psychic you will have to learn to be cautious in the delivery of your messages. You will have to learn to sort out what you can pass on and what you cannot. The truth is a very powerful weapon and not everyone is at a certain state of evolution to receive the truth.

You see, we are without physical handicap, unlike you, as our vision is not limited. Yes, we can see at times what lies ahead of you and we can tune into your chosen life path. We are able to give you hope and reassurance, trying to dispel the worries and confusion in your mind and to be a light on your dark horizon, but there are times when we cannot, for we would not be allowed to. We know it would hinder you to know what lies ahead. There are times when you have to have faith that all will be well, that in spite of all the obstacles and darkness that surrounds you, you will have to learn to be light and hope, but at other times we just cannot get through to you. There are moments when we know that your earthly life could be cut short because of your ignorance and we desperately try to break through to reassure you that there is no need to despair, all will be well, the future will be brighter. You are surrounded by darkness and a fog which we cannot penetrate and very often in those cases, we are able to get through via other people on earth who are receptive and who are light, then we hope they will pass on the messages of comfort and hope to you. So you see you are never forgotten or alone.

Now, for instance, as a psychic you may have with you a soul in despair, a soul who wants to be reassured that tomorrow will be brighter. You see this brightness, you see them as a gossamer light, you see them as spirit, laughing, young, full of vitality. You see them in spirit and with spirit, just as spirit. Will you tell them? Will you tell them even though it is the truth, "you are going into spirit by tomorrow or soon?" How many are ready to receive that? Very few have reached that stage on their path of evolution. So you can say with conviction and truth, "all will be well, there is a better life ahead," and they can leave your presence uplifted, strengthened, not filled with fear but with hope, yet unaware that their physical life is soon to cease. They will share this information with others how much hope they have been given and how much it has helped them, and within a short space of time they pass into their new life, to the spirit life. Now those who are cynics could be even more cynical. They were told of a better life and now they are dead, and they could become bitter and resentful because that is not what they wanted to happen to their loved one. They wanted them there in the material life with them, and yet a person who was filled with love for that loved one and only wanted what was best for them, will rejoice and will say with conviction that they are in a better life now, for that is the only reality. Eternity!

To be a possessor of psychic gifts and to be a receiver of the truth is a great responsibility and when you pass this on, when word spreads that you are a good receiver of psychic truth and evidence, people will come to you. You will be praised, and then another little demon will raise its head. Your ego will then preen itself and purr like a well fed kitten when the words of praise are heaped upon it. You will feel tall and powerful for you are the possessor of a great gift and you will use it and you will give and give the information you receive. The more accolade heaped upon you the bigger that little demon inside you grows. It wants more, it wants to be fed.

There will be monetary rewards. You will obtain material riches you never possessed before. Your vanity will be fed, you are able to purchase garments that were out of your reach, you will be surrounded by objects of luxury in your environment and all the time this monster within you grows because it has a hunger that cannot be assuaged. If that is what you want, then it is yours, but it is only ballast you carry with you. There is no spiritual value in it whatsoever. You have chosen to be a psychic. You want to be a success, you want to be adored and praised and you want material riches? Then go and get them, let it be. It is your path, it is your life, you have chosen it.

If you have chosen instead to live and give generously, to make yourself available as a receiver of psychic truths and evidence, without realising it you have entered the path of spiritual service as well, for you will be honest and if there is an emptiness during your tuning in period you will admit to it. You will realise how wonderful it is to be part of this family of man and the Fatherhood of God. Your spirit will bubble with joy when a smile appears on a face that only minutes before has been in despair and tear stained. When tears of despair are replaced by tears of joy and love and you can feel the love of loved ones around them which almost chokes you with the emotions they bring, the love that fills you threatening to overpower you, when weariness is replaced by vitality and purpose, when the "thank you" and the blessing you receive from the sitter has more power than any monetary reward, the feeling of having been a giver of truth and love being sufficient upon itself, then you have done well. You have chosen well, because you are in charge, you have no glamour in your life that could so easily rule you, for you have smiled tolerantly upon the whispers of your ego that wanted to be told how wonderful you are and laughed it away, knowing that the feeling of love is more important, that the service you are able to give is reward enough.

So choose my friend, choose according to your need and may your own spirit lead you into a path that is necessary for your own spiritual evolution.

CHAPTER 8

THE WISDOM OF THE OLD

The Wise
Have still the keeping of their proper peace,
Are guardians of their own tranquillity.
Wordsworth

We bring God's love, the universal God, whose breath is in every living thing created by Him, the Great Spirit. As we straighten up with our head held high to look heavenwards, symbolically we raise our thought vibrations to give thanks. With arms outstretched and palms upwards, we feel the life pulsating in our body recharging itself. We thank you, Great Spirit, for the light of the sun which warms our body, lightens our heart and stimulates the mind. We thank you for the light and the darkness, for the stars in the heavens which give us inspiration so that even in the darkness there is light. As the beautiful kaleidoscope of Nature's colours and vistas unfold before us we feel humble and grateful and we praise you for the beauty that is all around us. We give thanks with our spirit, for that is part of you. As we stand on the firm ground of Mother Earth, feeling her pulse beating against the soles of our feet, we thank her for the nourishment that is available to all, for Great Spirit, we respect all that is life. We are here to learn the lessons we have chosen and which are essential for our spiritual progress.

May we learn in humbleness to be true as we are created in your image. May we realise the equality of all life and learn to love without condition. May we learn to share all that is given to us with so much generosity, learn to accept, but not to judge our brother and to look beneath the skin to find the beauty that is created by you also.

Love makes us strong, invincible and just for, helped by the power of your love, we can share the lessons of life with others.

May the blessing of the sun, the moon, the stars and of Mother Earth envelop you in their warmth and in their magnificence. May love be your guide, your inspiration and your strength. Be true to all that comes from God. Be light. Be yourself.

The blessings of the Great Spirit will uplift you, strengthen you, guide your footsteps and in the darkness you will never be alone.

We would like to stress how important and vital it is in your life to be a good spiritual counsellor.

When I was incarnated into the physical world, and lived in our home at the foot of the great Rocky Mountains in the north of the Americas, we lacked for nothing. There was sufficient for everyone's need, spiritually and materially and spiritual awareness was within us. We revered the wisdom that our elders had gained in their experience of life for we knew we could talk to them, share our troubles with them and not one word of judgment would pass their lips.

Our ancestors were the ones that escaped the holocaust which destroyed Atlantis and Lemura. They had so much spiritual wisdom and yet there were those for whom this was not enough. They wanted the thrill that only physical power could give them, so they ignored the spiritual intellect and brought about the destruction of something that could have been heaven on earth.

We used to get strength and inspiration by listening to the vibrations and the sounds of Mother Earth who is so rich in wisdom. If you would listen and observe you, too, can learn from this, learning to respect the fruits of the Earth so that as you raise your eyes towards the light and the warmth of the sun you will be filled with joy and give thanks for that light. In the dark you can feel alone but when the golden light of the moon appears and you see the lights twinkling you can observe the vastness of the universe. Then you will feel humble, yet great to be part of the Great Spirit, but when you are young, eager, impulsive and hungry for material success, all this awesome wisdom disappears into the background of your mind for the glitter of success has a stronger lure than the creation of the Great Spirit. So it was amongst us. The younger brothers could not wait to grow into manhood. They wanted to be men before they had the wisdom and strength to be so. Impatiently they used to rush into the tents of the elders imploring them to give them weapons so they could go out to hunt the big buffalo, to prove their strength and their power over man and beast.

The elders in their wisdom pointed out that not everyone is ready to be the possessor of the truth and to be in charge of a weapon that could end a physical life. Taking away the temple that houses the soul is a great responsibility and should not be undertaken lightly and to hunt and kill the big brown cow was something not to be done superficially just for the thrill of it. The young hunter should show respect for the big buffalo, should apologise to its spirit and the spirit of the buffalo will understand, for every part of him will be used and will be a necessity in prolonging the physical life. The elders used to talk of respect for all life, of the necessity to take time to think and they were the ones who gently and wisely pointed out the wonders of the universe, of all creation. They listened patiently to the outpourings and desires of the young ones, knowing that in place of their impatience and despair, there was a greater love waiting for them, a love so great that it would change their lives for ever and make them invincible. But when you are young, you only want what you can see, can feel and touch, and when you are young the only reality is the one you can see, feel and hear. You have no desire to be still, to listen and observe the only reality of life.

Yet in many cases the elders managed to get through to the young impatient mind and to the troubled soul. As we observe your world today, we see how it is lacking in the wisdom of the elders with their ability to listen with love and compassion. When you are able just to listen to someone in trouble and let them free themselves of despair and confusion, they can then see where they are erring and have a clearer vision of where they have to go and what they should do in order to retain their spiritual and mental balance.

Everyone, if they wish, can be a spiritual counsellor if they have the ability to be a good listener, to fill their hearts and minds with love and compassion. Do not judge, for there is no need. The troubled spirit who comes to you for advice and help already knows that somewhere they have lost sight of the right path, so there is no need for judgment because they are already judging themselves. With your love, compassionate silence and listening ear you can show them where they have erred, without uttering one word of condemnation. That has always been a good strong basis for spiritual counselling.

The willingness to listen is greatly needed. Already there are organisations in your world who compassionately and patiently listen to troubled minds. With this compassionate silence they often manage to avoid the shortening of a physical life which would then be deprived of learning the lessons they had chosen to experience, for it is absolutely unnecessary for a spirit to be constantly troubled.

That is not your mission in life nor part of your destiny. You are here to pay the debts of past misdemeanours in past lives, for you are an honourable spirit and have chosen to do so, but the law of mercy which is your spiritual counsellor will guide you, showing the way to spiritual enlightenment and joy. We found that joy long ago in the beauty of the Great Spirit's creation. We found the strength from the sun, the moon, the stars and we never ceased to give thanks for the bountiful fruits and the life that Mother Earth gave to us.

There are so many elders in your life who are ignored and who shrivel away when their wisdom is ignored. They are patiently waiting to rejoin their ancestors in the spiritual world for they feel they have nothing else to give and are a burden, yet your old are so rich, in wisdom and you shut them away and ignore them. Take them out of their corners, let them talk and listen to them for they have so much to give. When their time comes to rejoin their loved ones in their spiritual home, they won't go with disappointment, bitterness and resentment or with a feeling of futility, they will go strong, knowing they have respect, knowing they have done well, that they are needed and are still part of the thriving living community. Listen to the wisdom of the old then you too, one day, could be a spiritual counsellor, a bringer of wisdom and experience and you will look forward to growing old, rather than dreading it.

May the light and the warmth of the sun shine upon you. May in the darkness of the night the golden light of the moon enhance your darkness. May the stars be the pathfinder in the way you have chosen and may the fruits of the earth be bountiful.

May the Great Spirit bless you, not just now but always.

RELATIONSHIPS AND SPIRITUAL GROWTH

Have love; not love alone for one,
But man as man thy brother call,
And scatter like the circling sun
Thy charities on all.

Schiller

Why are there so many intricacies in relationships? The human spirit can learn and can absorb many experiences in order to grow. This is part of the evolvement of the spirit as we are here to evolve, for that is our quest. It is a crusade the human spirit embarks upon when it enters into another incarnation.

Each relationship is important whether it be between parents and children, brothers and sisters, husbands and wives or between friends. Each has something to teach us if we let it. The whole human race has been founded on these relationships. We all need a complimentary being in our lives to make us feel complete and we are always looking for this other half to give us a feeling of oneness. Sometimes we have chosen to live in certain incarnations without the physical presence of that twin soul in our life and when we do it is with the understanding of learning a lesson. In that case there will be an inner loneliness in the absence of the other half. The spirit always reaches out, searching and looking for that completeness, but in our search for that other half we very often neglect other equally important relationships. In spite of the existence of that other half which gives us this inner completeness, there are many other affinities in our life, people we feel comfortable and at ease with and a sense of familiarity which is not easily explained. Affinities touch our lives many times and although we cannot, or do not wish to separate ourselves from them, they make an interesting pattern and are part of the jigsaw we call life, with a capital L. Many books are written about what life is all about, trying to give meaning or a spiritual substance to it and many more will be written in this quest, in order to give us some kind of answer to the meaning of life.

What does give us substance in life? Many souls incarnate and find life wanting. They isolate themselves from the human race, they live in total isolation or a hermitic existence because they find it difficult and troublesome to relate to other human souls. They also realise that only in isolation can they be at peace and in harmony, but that is an easy option. However, we have to leave the choice to each individual because if you have chosen to seal yourself off from the rest of the human race, that is your choice because you have chosen to experience living in isolation without any human contact. You even agreed that this is the way you want to serve God by severing all relationships, to live your three score and ten years or so in this state of existence. Hopefully, you will have learned by the time of your return home to your source, your spiritual abode. You will then realise that this is only part of an answer and that coping with relationships is very important in your spiritual growth.

To be at peace with yourself you will have to accept yourself with all the flaws in your spiritual, mental and physical make-up. You see yourself wanting and you realise that the answer lies within yourself. In order to grow you need to share your experiences with the rest of your fellowmen, or a particular few you have chosen to be with in this specific life. You will hear the saying that, "It is give and take in all relationships." One has to work hard in a relationship, but there are those which seem to take no effort at all. Those are the ones who have an affinity with your spiritual self, where you can be yourself as you don't have to prove anything to them. They know you and accept you as you accept them. There is mutual acceptance and when you come to that realisation, you have indeed grown within those particular relationships.

Now what about those where there is a clashing of personalities, where you find you have to prove at all times you are either superior or equal to them in a mental, spiritual and very often a physical way. What about those? When you reach a certain stage of acceptance where there is complete understanding, where you let go of the strings that tie you to each other and only thought waves of love emanate from you to them, then you have reached a state of evolution where great spiritual strides forward have been made. You will also realise that you have eternity to prove who you really are but others have not yet reached that stage. The material and physical severance of emotional ties can be painful, but with that pain a great cleansing process will take place. Like Phoenix rising out of the ashes, a brighter and better spiritual existence will emerge and with that you will realise it has been worthwhile.

Some of your relationships will work out to a satisfactory conclusion, sometimes only by total surrender of your real self which you will not realise until you shed your physical 'overcoat', the physical body. Surrender is not the answer, for you have 'given in'. You have been dominated, have been the passive partner in that relationship and your spirit's desire had to be suppressed. You were like a stagnant pond and underneath the calm surface a sort of rotting had to set in. People in those conditions are beset by disease and physical ill health because they are not allowed to grow or stretch themselves, for there will be disharmony between the mind, body and spirit where diseases set in.

All human ills are caused by a disassociation between the body and spirit. There is no accidental illness, accident, or any unwellness which does not have its cause in a disassociation between body and spirit. In your emotional state when you are unable to be in touch with your higher consciousness, your psyche is disturbed by the strong emotions that rage within you and in that case you manipulate with your own psychicness to receive answers which are destructive to yourself in order to justify your actions and behaviour and to justify your present existence.

Why do human spirits let themselves be dominated, why do they let themselves stagnate? They tell themselves it is all for a peaceful life, but your incarnation is for growth. In a human incarnation, you are given a choice to grow and you choose a particular path which will help in your growth. You will meet many people and you will have relationships which are all essential for your growth. There is no accidental meeting. People often exclaim "what a co-incidence meeting you or hearing from you." There is no such thing as co-incidence. Everything is part of a plan where you will eventually reach that stage of evolution which will make you at one with the infinite. No matter how humble your occupation or how humble you think your job may be, it is the path you have chosen. It is of no consequence whether you have decided to follow an intellectual, academic or a medical profession, or to be a refuse collector, butcher, baker, candlestick maker, or even if you throw yourself at the mercy of your fellowmen by standing on the corner to beg, you have chosen it and are given chances to evolve at all levels.

It is true, man cannot live by bread alone. You need spiritual food as you need physical food. You decide what you feed your physical body or your taste buds will discern what will agree with you, but how do you choose your spiritual food? You choose this according to what your spiritual taste buds are ready to accept or reject. There are many things that you will get a chance to absorb on a spiritual level and you will find it very difficult to accept. You might have chosen an incarnation where anything of a metaphysical nature or of mysticism is totally unacceptable to you. You might have chosen an orthodox path, to follow a certain doctrine or religious organisation so that you may learn. You might have chosen to incarnate into an Islamic incarnation where a husband can choose as many wives as he wishes. In that case, you have chosen the lesson of sharing. You have to learn to accept that you do not own anyone and what better way than to share with other wives the love and attention of a male person in this, particular incarnation. You might have chosen an incarnation where the divorce laws are so rigid that even in spite of those laws, you have chosen intimate relationships with the opposite sex and to come to terms with those laws, to rise above them or come to the realisation that the rigidity of those laws are not for you, that the partners you have chosen and who are trying to dominate or possess you (which is against all spiritual natural law) are not for you. You break free, for it is essential for your growth.

Then why do we get so restless when we are in a human incarnation? Why do we search for various directions? We have to remember that when we incarnate here in order to experience human relationships which start from the second we enter into this life and make our first human contact – the mother's womb, that this is the first important relationship. How can we throw off the chains where there is total dominance where we feel stifled and retarded in our spiritual and mental growth? How can we throw off the shackles? It is a vicious circle where sometimes we might have to depend on the one person that is dominating us, who has power over us. Spiritually we can not be dominated, for no-one can put the chains on our spirit. We are free spiritually and we are equal, for we each have the same chances.

A cry from this planet goes out into the etheric world, "God help me," from unhappy spirits who are cohabiting with other spirits and are miserable, without hope and desolate. Depression and illness overshadows their lives and their cries for help are desperate. We would like to say to those, throw off the chains. If you are in a situation where physically you are unable to sever all the ties, remember that spiritually you can, for they cannot touch you. The instant you realise that you cannot be dominated in this way, a healing process will take place. This healing will come from within, brought on by your acceptance, and once the spirit who is trying to dominate you realises this, it cannot touch you or possess you. Even the physical power might wane and your spiritual self realises that it is free.

Draw inspiration from those who were incarnated in the physical, how their faith rose above their chains, and their great spirits felt free. They loved in abundance and whatever happened to them physically could not touch the freedom of their spiritual self.

A mother who tries to hang on to the umbilical cord of the infant long past their childhood and adolescence cannot hold back the spirit of that child. In cases where we are held back through the environment we have chosen and convention forces us to observe those rules, it is a wise spirit who realises that certain rules and laws have to be observed. The human mind needs a certain form of discipline so as to lead an orderly and well regulated life, yet spiritually, no matter where and no matter who you are, you are free.

When Jesus was crucified, his body was mutilated, yet his spirit was untouched and it will always be so. Great human spirits have walked these paths and they are inspiring you now. Take heart from their lives, for they rose above all adverse human conditions and that is what made them great. Remember Einstein? He was regarded as a dunce at school and ridiculed. The simplest facts of mathematics were beyond him and yet he made great contributions to mankind. Albert Schweitzer tried to bring a certain light to Africa, but soon realised that some of these ideals were slightly misguided. He was an inspiration to many people as he tried to help and did help in many ways, for what man has yet to learn is that each culture has to find their own way and the law of compassion should be used, regardless of colour or creed.

It is part of our duty to give assistance to make a material life more bearable, for it is in giving that we receive. Very often when we are on this path of giving and are involved in relationships where there is a giver and a taker, we find that the giving on the part of the giver has become like a drug, for the giver realises that it is only by giving as much as he or she is able to, they reach a certain stage of mental exhilaration. They can only achieve this state, so they have come to believe, by constantly giving, even when it is pointed out to them that their giving is not always appreciated or at times even harmful. The giver needs that stimulation because they are by then out of balance spiritually and mentally.

We can just imagine that you will say, you say that it is in giving you will receive – why should we not give then? Should we not give if somebody asks us or begs us for assistance? Yes, we should always give what we have – an unlimited supply of love – but how can a spirit grow that is assisted constantly in its striving? How can a spirit evolve that is constantly upheld by others, where every problem they come across is removed by someone else so that the spirit is being retarded. Is that what it is all about, to retard one another? Is that what the Nazarene meant when he said "love one another". In order to understand you have to realise that when He was nailed to the cross, confined into the physical body, having to feel the pain, His cry of anguish, "Father why has thou forsaken me?" was that of a mortal soul, for He is mortal, but when the spirit disengaged itself from the physical vehicle which had served Him, He was free of the chains. His Ministry goes on. He walks among you now, again a vehicle, unrecognised, finding the human race unchanged; a giver of love, an observer yet at the same time totally involved in the service of God because He has realised that all relationships, involve God.

What you are here to learn from the relationships is that we should love as God loves us – He lets us decide, He lets us choose, He does not judge us. He does not criticise us for He knows his laws are just. He is the Omnipotent presence, the spark of life, is Love. When realisation dawns on us that we are here to learn to love like God, not because someone does us a favour and we have to return this, but because we are part of God and longing to be at one with Him. With that awakening, our relationships can work. Adversity will disappear and not only will we love like God, we shall be like Him. Where there is darkness there will be light. Where there is ignorance there will be understanding. Where there was despair there will be hope and in the end, there will only be love.

RELATIONSHIPS II

If people would whistle more and argue less, the world would be much happier and probably just as wise.

Book of Wisdom

There are so many different kinds of relationships and the weaknesses in any personality are the ones where there is the desire to own and to possess. That does not just include your material possessions, your houses, cars, furnishings, object d'art or whatever your heart desires or thinks necessary for everyday comfort, it extends to human personalities and animal life. The sense of possession induces narrow mindedness and we have a terrible sense of loneliness and anger when someone else tries to make claim on our possessions.

You can have it all, if you wish, by giving freedom to all those who touch your life, whether in the form of friendship, relatives or marital bonds. It is within freedom that you receive the most precious gift, and the perfect example of this is He, the Creator who created you, gave you life and loves you overwhelmingly, for you are His child, but despite this, you are free to choose whether you acknowledge it or not. With the majority of souls there is the desire to be close to the giver of life and love, in order to return to the warmth of that love and that loving embrace. Why else should there be so many different creeds and philosophies? Why else do men go out looking to fulfil the longing within? Why else are there so many books written about this subject, the mystery of life? It is the reality of life and love and in this freedom we can find love.

When we are trying to tie another life to us, whether it is with emotional blackmail by saying, "If you leave me I think I shall die," or, "I can't live without you," or by burdening your loved ones, friends and associates constantly with your tales of woe and your apparent immense suffering so you evoke pity in them rather than love, these would be negative bonds. Every time they want to cut loose, the pity and the guilt that ties them to you will hold them back. By letting go you will have a vast circle of friends who will think of you with love and affection. Your relatives will come to you out of love and when they want to. Loved ones will seek you with love, not with a sense of duty or guilt. Only the one bond built out of freedom and generosity, will be a true bond and that can span many miles. No boundaries and no distance will be big enough to cut that bond, nor will you ever feel lonely because you will feel that love wherever you are and whoever you are.

Many times you look up, attracted by the joyful singing of the birds as they soar high, and part of you longs to be one of them. Well, if you use your imagination you can be by thinking you are those birds for you, too, can sing joyfully in your freedom and soar high.

When the loved ones who are dear to you in love and affection go through a harrowing time, you must realise that they have chosen this particular experience to learn. Now, you will ask the question, "Was I not told to love my fellow man as myself? Was I not told that to give service or to give help is one of the noblest things to do in my earthly incarnation?" Of course, by sharing your love with that person, by offering yourself in service to help carry the burden that weighs them down at that particular time, you are doing one of the noblest things in the path of human evolution. You are helping them to carry the cross which weighs them down. One man stepped out of the multitude and said to the Nazarene as the nails and the weight of the cross bore down on Him, "Master, let me carry your cross." One out of the multitude who He had helped, loved and cared for! When there is just one person who steps forward with love and offers to help share your cross, accept it with love. Do not turn them away, for you give them a chance to serve and to progress. Be proud, be grateful. The Nazarene knew that nobody could carry that cross, for He alone had to do it, but the thought that there was one soul willing to share His burden and the joy this thought brought to Him, gave Him the strength to carry His cross.

When you enter into a marital bond, whatever country you live in and no matter what your laws, you offer to share your love, your joys, your sorrow, your pain and your material wealth. When you agree to bring a new life forward and give it a chance to grow nearer its source, the Creator, you guide and protect it in the years when that life is vulnerable or easily influenced and you do it to the best of your ability, for you know that your child or children will at times have to learn through experience because that is the only way. You will be there, and you love your child whether that child is worthy of your love or not; the question does not arise in the mind because you have a special bond. If you are wise and generous enough with your love, you can share in their sorrow but you will make no attempt to take that sorrow away from them. You share it by being there, loving them without overwhelming them, a symbol of love and strength. In time they will realise that you cannot take that suffering from them, but by your strength you give them comfort, hope and love.

So it is in all your relationships. How many times do you hear the words "fellow man" or "You can choose your friends, but you cannot choose your relatives?" When you have reached awareness, knowing that in this vast universe life and the so-called mystery of life, goes on and on and on for there is no end, you will realise that you have been very wise in choosing your awkward relatives or those you call contrary and difficult. It is easy and convenient to choose the ones we are compatible with, those who are amenable. How wonderful! for there always will be those with whom you are totally at ease, but what about those who set your teeth on edge, who make you scream out silently in frustration and anger, those where every meeting ends in an argument? Now they are a true challenge. Why are they there? You picked them. You chose to be near them, so what are you going to do about it? The same principle applies – give them freedom, the freedom to choose their way and love them regardless. They will test your patience constantly, but your love is invincible because you now have realised you are part of God, you *are* God, because being part of Him you are Him. You can shout joyfully, "I am God, I am part of Him." Your love does not change. Like God, you love eternally. However difficult a relationship, it cannot touch you with negativity as you know that you are part of God, you are that love.

Especially now at this particular time when once again the circle of human relationships has reached a point where some people are over-satiated, many of them have multiple relationships and many marital bonds, where they try again and again, only to find that each one they enter into is fraught with difficulties. There are men and women who are determined to get it right, but why at this particular time in the eighties and nineties are there so many divorces, too many breakups of relationships?

There are several explanations for this. Remember that here in your Western civilisation you have now found a way to control your population, but because of wars in the past, many souls are looking for a chance to reincarnate on Earth. There is Central India where the population multiplies drastically and where birth control has not yet got a strong hold. The incarnations are much harder there because the philosophy of reincarnation is deeply embedded in them and some of the people have now tried to embrace ideas of Western ideology. Their belief of reincarnation, without Christ's law of compassion, narrows down the field of earthly experience. It is a big country and people are incarnating into the Western civilisation in order to have the chance to have several relationships, which is one of the reasons why we have an almost epidemic occurrence of multiple marriages. The fact they have chosen so many will give them a chance to pay off some Karmic debts. Again, it is a personal choice. More people have chosen to be on Earth at this particular period, for the time is drawing close when there will be an incident, which will be a catalyst and a new thought wave will overshadow the human race where people in general will learn to use their mental faculties and psychic gifts. Extrasensory perception will be the norm rather than the exception and that will be the age of awakening. It is not until this great metamorphosis has occurred that a new era will dawn. All the people who have raced through this particular life in the twentieth century will have accumulated knowledge and the experience in order to be of help and assistance to those that are confused and bewildered after this incident has occurred. It is no wrath of God, but due to the law of cause and effect, the result of man's ignorance. Do not despair because a shining bright new ideology will rise out of it.

In your relationships, whether you have multiple relationships or whether you have chosen to be in a singular one, each one can teach you something of importance. If a friend ceases to be your friend, you should realise that the friendship was there for the time it was needed and there will be others who will fill a need, as you will for them. If there is a change of partner, try not to cling to the past. Look at what you have learned and give thanks to that partner for he or she were instrumental in helping you to grow spiritually and mentally. Everything that happens in your life is there to help you and to give you realisation that you are a free spirit. Respect the spirit in your fellow man, no matter what relationship they are to you for you are related to all your fellow men because of God, whether you call Him God or you call Him by another name – just remember His real name is Love.

Where there is darkness – and this planet Earth is dark – every thought of light and love is necessary to brighten it. As you brighten your home with flowers and colours, brighten this world with thoughts of love, peace and light.

When you are being overshadowed and somebody tries to force their ideas on you, you don't have to accept them. Unfortunately that is why it was necessary to stamp out with force the evil that existed on Earth over fifty years ago. This evil, this anti-Christ which murdered and killed people for their different beliefs or because they belonged to a different race, had to be fought with force, to be cut out like a cancerous growth before it could get hold and spread. Like many forms of cancer it still has metastases breaking out which have to be attacked and destroyed.

So, fight with love, fight with light. No darkness can penetrate the light of God, only the light can overshadow the darkness.

Next tine you visit your awkward relatives, just remember you chose them for a reason.

REINCARNATION

One should never feel resentment against men, never judge them, because of the recollection of an act of malice, for we do not know all the good that at other times they have been sincerely willed and achieved; undoubtedly the evil pattern that we have once and for all observed will come back, but the soul is much richer than that it has other patterns also which will return.

Proust

What do we really mean when we talk of reincarnation? That in some past life you, as a person, have lived as an Egyptian pharaoh, Roman centurion or French revolutionary? That you, with your twentieth-century memory, can look back on and remember your rebirths? This is a dream that many of us have, an experience we long to undergo. The real truth is far more mysterious, far grander. It is our true inner selves, our innate characters, which reflect those past lives and it is through spiritual and metaphysical disciplines that we can be aided in recollecting them.

(Taken from the book *Reincarnation* by Hans Stefan Santessan).

This spirit world is your real home. It is from this world that the spirit embarks to start yet another physical incarnation. It is the route of all spirit. Life starts here, divided by several planes of existence and those that live in the highest plane rejoice when a spirit sheds another overcoat, after the lessons have been learned. This refining process brings the spirit closer to its source and touches others with its refined vibration. When we have mastered and conquered some of our more base emotions, we actually help the members of our spiritual family on their path of spiritual evolution.

Once again we are touching the subject of reincarnation. More and more people who are seeking and searching are realising that past, present and future are linked together. Past lives, past incarnations have a great influence on the present and on the future, because our past lives shape our innerself and give us a sense of direction and a very profound purpose in all our lives. So, we each choose an existence which will give us the most chances, to work off the Karma which we incurred during all our other existences, no matter what gender it occurred in.

In many cases it would be helpful if psychologists could accept the theory of reincarnation, for the psyche very often carries some of the more negative aspects of past lives over to another life.

Again, we have chosen one particular life as an example because we are more familiar with that life. In this case we are able to draw conclusions and draw attention to the fact that some of the lessons are being learned at this particular moment in time.

We have to go back in time to the period referred to in history as the medieval time, for this spirit existed in a medieval castle, which was everything one could think of as a medieval castle. That castle was in the heart of England and yet Ireland is another country that seems to touch this life in a strong Karmic way. It only touched this life in this particular lifetime briefly by association with people who have been born in Ireland (or the Emerald Isle which is a far prettier and far more apt name for it). We want to talk about England, yet Ireland comes into this specific life. This spirit who was then in a female incarnation, was being brought up as a much loved and spoilt child of her father, the only daughter, but there were also two brothers. The mother died in giving birth to this child, so all the love that the father had within him was bestowed upon her. (Yes, her father was in this lifetime as well). There was then a bond formed between father and daughter, a bond that will never be broken, can never be severed, a strong spiritual bond, but the love was very obsessive on the father's side in many ways. He was intent upon not having his beloved daughter's innocence spoiled by any outsider, so she was surrounded by love and harmony, but in a very isolated existence as everything was tested and vetted by the father before being allowed into the vicinity of the daughter. The two brothers indulged their beloved sister and between the three existed the bond of friendship and good fellowship. Again, these two young men have entered into her present life – one is a present son and the other one is a cousin – and there is that love and friendship still existing from the moment the three lives made contact with one another.

The daughter grew into a fragile, almost etheric beauty. Her mind was unsullied and pure and she was very religious and devout. Adjacent to the castle was the chapel which the father had built for his wife and which was used frequently by the daughter. Many hours were spent in prayer and meditation and as she gazed at the carved images of the Nazarene in the chapel she had many beautiful visions. She was particularly drawn to the figure of Jesus and the Christ spirit, feeling very close to the peace and at one with the Christ.

Unfortunately, the father's lifetime came to an end without him having achieved what he wanted to achieve, the perfect suitor for his beloved daughter. On his death-bed, she had to promise him to stay pure, to devote her life to prayer and only to give herself in pure love to a man whose mind was like hers. Of course, the daughter was devastated by the death of her father; she was drained, desolate and overcome by depressions. The light seemed to have gone out of her life. But, like all the young, youth asserted itself and she started to become aware of her surroundings again, to look longingly out, hoping that from somewhere, someone would come and take her hand and lead her into a life with love and with joy.

From history which is a bit tarnished and not always correct, we are fairly aware of what went on during these times. People were travelling and news was passed from mouth to mouth. The daughter's etheric beauty and her purity were well known amongst the local men and known even across the borders to the Celtic regions. Many a noble soul came calling in order to obtain the hand in marriage of this lady, but none of them seemed to stir her. She was waiting to give herself to a noble pure mind as she had promised her father.

On this, particular night, a young man in his early twenties, from a noble but not very rich family in Ireland, accompanied by a small entourage, was seeking adventure. He travelled, seeking to fight for whoever would hire him, fighting for a cause and, in exchange for monetary award, was willing to fight for hire. He was endowed with great physical looks, immense charm and many a lady swooned at the sight of him, being overcome by his charming manner, as he had indeed the gift to make a woman feel wonderful and wanted. This young man, in his travels, had heard of our lady and he was determined to meet her. Not only was he impressed by the stories about her beauty and purity, he was also impressed by her dowry at the completion of the marriage contract. He knew he had to impress her brothers with daring and bravery in order to win the fair lady and he managed to obtain an invitation to the castle whilst a banquet was going on, He then realised he could make the lady blush, to be flustered and unsure. He received an invitation to stay as he had proved himself proficient at the jousting and all the sports young men at that time indulged in. As he was good company and good fun, the brothers saw no reason to refuse an invitation and he used that time to woo the lady. He was a charmer and because her life was very solitary, as prior to her father's death she was spoilt and protected, the presence of this young man was like a breath of fresh air which gave her the joie de vivre that she needed, lifting her spirits and making her feel young and carefree. Yet, she still prayed regularly, attending the services in the chapel, and hoped that this was the love and the life she was looking for. The young man had impressed not only the daughter of the house, but the two brothers as well with his daring skill and charming, easy going manner. When he asked for the lady's hand in marriage he was totally honest about his lack of monetary funds, but he offered his services, his skills and a life of devotion. He was accepted, but he was in that particular incarnation an opportunist which came out of necessity as there had always been lack of funds even though he was of noble blood, realising he had to live by his wits in order to survive and gain entry into the other noble houses.

The wedding was held, was greatly celebrated and all seemed well at first with the newly formed relationships, but the young woman started to feel uneasy. She was longing to hold a baby in her arms. She wanted a family because there was so much love in her which she wanted to share and she wanted a child to whom she could give the mother love that she never had which she felt so absolutely necessary in forming and shaping a new life. Her new husband at once thought that, now there was no need to worry about lack of funds, he could indulge in daring adventures, riding away on crusades and he also had another very obsessive emotion which was that of jealously, being very possessive. So instead of the woman's life expanding and meeting more people so having more life experiences, she became even more isolated and when her husband went away on his adventures and crusades she was kept virtually incarcerated in her castle, more lonely than ever. She sat at her spinning wheel, spinning, singing sad songs and still a longing in her, realising that her dreams had not been fulfiled. Her consolations were her prayers, her meditations, her communication with God, as she called it and with the Christ spirit. She wrote down thoughts and the songs that formed in her head. She made many garments, spinning and weaving the cloths herself, keeping herself occupied as best she could, longing and looking out, surveying the countryside around her, knowing that was her life existence. As it was the custom then, she was even forced to wear a chastity belt. Thus she was not only spiritually chained, she was physically chained and all the time there was this great longing in her to be free. This went on for many years and it was not until the fifteenth year of their marriage that after her husband had returned from one of his crusades, she conceived a child and after a premature labour gave birth to a son. She was not very strong and although the son survived, the mother died. Her unhappy spirit had weakened her frail physical body and she joined her beloved father in her real home because that is the reality of the world of spirit.

Now that particular existence has been the interloper in the present life of this spirit. There have been and still are great moments of loneliness, this feeling of being incarcerated and chained down. The greatest aversion this particular spirit has in this life is being forced to be in a place where she does not want to be. There have been moments of great depression and longing to break free. That is why in this life she takes long walks surrounded by nature, then the spirit is happy and content, and when the spirit is with like-minded people whose mentality is on the same plane, there is contentment and peace. Any obsessive love that is overpowering and chains its life down is harming the physical because when the spirit withdraws from trying to be dominated, it affects the physical and takes then the form of disease or illness, because all illnesses come from an unhappy spirit. A healthy, happy spirit will create a healthy body.

So, the lesson is not only for this spirit to learn not to be dominated, but that we have a choice. That choice is not always apparent or made easy, but it is each spirit's divine gift from its creator to choose its own path. Those who are in the vicinity and touch the life of that spirit are there by choice for they have chosen to learn their lessons, just as we choose lessons because we have come into the orbit or surroundings of a particular spirit or spirits. All the people we are in close contact with, or people who leave a great impression on our minds, all help in our learning. They help us to work off our Karma so that we are a step nearer to our goal. In all these experiences we have which we often view with a very negative attitude of mind where we say, "I could have done without this and I would rather have had that," we have actually gone through a sort of cleansing process where we are wiping the slate clean. All is there for a purpose, no experience, no matter how trivial you think it is, is without its purpose and we learn from them all if we are willing to. The thing to avoid is that of self-pity because this is the emotion that suppresses our spiritual energies. If we can look at our experiences as an observer, saying, "we have learned another lesson," then we have learned how to cope with this particular negative emotion, how to overcome it, how to rise above it. Things are difficult because we are in the physical, held down and held to convention by man-made laws. These are necessary in the physical environment because we have not yet mastered our emotions and the disciplines of the man-made laws are guidelines to channel our emotions and teach us the disciplines so necessary for future spiritual existence

No spirit has the right, objectively thinking, to suppress another. We all have the right to choose our own particular way which we feel gives us the much needed peace and spiritual contentment we are seeking. We might not agree if members of our family choose a particular creed or spiritual philosophy, but we have to learn to accept that that particular one is right for them if they feel it is so at any given moment. So we learn the lesson of acceptance and learn to accept not to oppress our loved ones with an overpowering, domineering, possessive love. Love should set us free, it is given freely to us and we should give it without condition. Those we love we should set free with our love, not chain them down. It is painful for any parent to watch their offspring very often walk into disaster or suffer painful experiences but, filled with love, we should realise that those experiences are necessary so that the spirit grows in order to reach a spiritual maturity. Parents are, in a way, the representatives of God, the omnipotent parent of all compassion and love. It is a big responsibility to be in charge, to be a guiding influence to a new life entering into a physical existence. Many parents are overawed by it. We are duty bound to give them guidance, to teach them control of all emotions, teach them to bring out the kind and loving spiritual warmth that is in all life and to show them by example to have respect for all life and at certain times to set them free, let them stretch themselves. "Do unto others."

But, besides your physical relatives you have your spiritual ones, the ones who have chosen to incarnate outside your blood-relative ties, so they touch your lives which rekindles an old spiritual bond. With some of them you feel good in their presence, but with others you recoil as your spirit and higher self remembers, but please try to remember that whenever any of these emotions overcome you, all have something to offer. All who touch you in some way are there for a purpose.

This life, the life we are writing about, had to learn to break free, not to let herself be ruled, not to let herself be spoilt and possessed but to walk tall and free and learn to love freely and let go. There are many chains, spiritual chains, that hold her down and sometimes they are harder and more difficult to shake off than the physical ones because they have been with her for such a long time.

So when you feel you are overcome by loneliness, by a feeling of being chained down and oppressed, remember it is your right to be free. That is the God-given right, given to you gracefully by a loving, giving God, the Father of the universe and He does not give anything with conditions, but it was given to you with love, out of love, for love's sake to set you free. So be free, be loving and realise you are a child of the universe, you have a right to be free for eternity.

REINCARNATION II

'Tis of the essence of life here,
Though we choose greatly, still to lack
The lasting memory at all clear,
That life has for us on the wrack.
Nothing but what we somehow chose;
Thus are we wholly stripped of pride
In the pain that has but one close,
Bearing it crushed and mystified.

Robert Frost

This time, different influences have come together to elaborate and delve deeper and we have chosen this one particular life to illustrate the fact of the science of reincarnation, which is a natural science, so we draw on the memory bank of a North American Indian. I am the spokesman. One finds it difficult to be articulate once again in the physical language, because the language we use is of such beauty, such melodious harmony, and grammar so irrelevant that we would rather concentrate on the contents, the beauty and the sincerity of the communication. We have to work with preciseness of the physical language, but I am convinced that we can nevertheless convey our message.

As you will hear me give a commentary on the events and introduction, I thought I would let you know and inform you what my existence on the earth plane used to be. I was a professor in Oxford and I taught in the pre-Raphaelite era. But now we are talking about the natural science of reincarnation.

I am now coming in the guise and in the form and the essence of an Indian. I used to belong to the Black Crow tribe. Our life was enhanced by the free style we were permitted to live, by the full appreciation and enjoyment of all the natural bounty that was around us. This woman child – for we are all children in the path of evolution – then lived in this environment and we lived in a sort of encampment. We woke up to the sound of happy birds singing. All our food was given to us by Mother Earth, the great giver and provider. All we obtained, we joyfully accepted and gave thanks for. Mother Earth has been badly abused in this century, but when we walked and lived in the great plains of North America, the earth was yet untainted and gratefully gave forth its fruits to nourish us. We walked hand in hand with the spirits of our ancestors as communcation between the two worlds was absolutely natural. Our education came forth in the knowledge of our ancestors. Stories, words and living habits were passed down from generation to generation. We sat at the feet of our wise men, their words and advice being respected and honoured, as we honoured all life. If we killed a deer, we apologised to its spirit and the spirit of the deer accepted the fact that its meat was giving us sustenance and that the skin was keeping us warm, for each life has a purpose to fulfill. Do not destroy the beauty of this planet. As Mother Earth has been tainted and abused, she is revolting against the obscene destruction that has been happening to her.

The life we talk about of this woman child was a free life and a joyous one, yet then, as it is now, when a hurt or a painful experience occurred, the spirit was inclined to withdraw. We roamed the plains together, two young braves, trying to prove to our family and friends and to ourselves that we were strong and invincible. We communicated with nature, not only with spirits that lived within the natural kingdom, but those of our ancestors. We respected all life and yet, this brave who is now this woman child, but was then my brother, even then possessed a stubborn streak, ignoring danger signals, not always following the advice of the older generation. Many chances and opportunities were missed because this stubbornness stood in the way of progress.

The event we are talking about is of a particular hunt when we had to go into the forest, up into the hills, to hunt buffalo. We knew of a particular place near a stream which was the resting place of the great brown cow, we called it. Armed with our weapons, our bodies oiled and covered with earth, the moisture of the earth kept our bodies supple and its dark toned stains made us as one with the earth. It also helped to disguise the human scent, as we were told by those who had walked the path before. We were excited, a great challenge was waiting for us for never again would we be in the same situation with the same first thrill as we confronted our first brown cow. We decided not to go on our beloved horses, but to walk stealthily to the resting place of the great buffalo. We sat around the camp fire the night before listening to the voices and the talking of our friends, the animals. Sleep would not come as we were filled with the thrill of the adventure ahead of us, for we knew there could also be great danger if we did not follow the advice of our elders. Sitting cross-legged by the fire, we passed the pipe between us which was filled with fragrant herbs and lulled us into a sense of well being and a tranquil mental state, for thus is the quality of those herbs. We swayed back and forwards chanting the words we were taught by the older ones, and we both saw at that particular moment in our mind's eye our adversary, the great buffalo, a powerful massive looking animal. We tried to be firm, we tried to obtain the mental state of absolute conviction that all would be well, yet we were fighting the negative emotion of fear, knowing how easily things could go wrong. As we opened our eyes, the fire was just a glow in the dark. We curled up in our deerskins, gave thanks to the Mother Earth and slept. When the sun came up and we could feel the vibrations of the animal footsteps beneath the Mother Earth, we prepared to get up. Fresh clumps of earth were collected to cover our bodies again. We faced the sun, bowed and gave thanks for the light and the warmth. We thanked the Great Spirit for protection and we asked our ancestors who had walked this path before to guide us on the path we had chosen. As we had been told not to partake of any eating of flesh, but a few berries and a few mouthfuls of clear mountain stream water, we heeded that advice and then set out.

We appeared to be, to the casual onlooker, calm and confident, two young boys on the threshold of their manhood, seeking to prove that they had reached the maturity of man. Every step was carefully taken, for Mother Earth is a powerful medium that carries forth vibrations and tremors and the sensitive ears of the hunted are always alert and ready to pick up the signals. We came to the edge of the forest – a glade it appeared to be – and we listened. The wind was carrying the scent of the buffalo to us and we knew they were close. The light was not yet very strong, which was working well for us. We checked the sharpness of our knives which were so sharp that we dare not even take them out for any length of time in case we scratch ourselves, drawing blood, and the smell of blood again would send a warning signal to the animals for we wanted to surprise them. Very slowly and steadily we went forward. The scent of the great brown cow got stronger and stronger and I could sense the fear and trembling of my brother, as he could feel mine. As I was the older of the two, I felt that I had to be stronger and more positive in all I did and I tried not to show my doubt. As we got closer we could see through the thicket the resting place of the great buffalo. We heard the heavy breathing, the snorting sounds they make, the swishing of their tails which sounded like a whip in the stillness of that morning. I motioned to my brother to have the bow very taut and the arrow ready, to start aiming as we both intended to aim for the eye of the great big bull. As we got our bows ready, the bull turned his head and looked directly in our direction. At that instant I heard a fluttering to my left, saw the arrow fall to the ground and my brother turn round to flee, and swiftly and quickly he disappeared through the glade to leave me alone facing the great buffalo. As I was so close, I had no choice but to confront. I only managed to wound the animal before the rest of the herd came charging towards me.

Thus I found myself in the hunting ground of my ancestors, to join them. No bitterness or sadness was in my spirit or in my thoughts. All these things were only felt for my brother, for I know what possessed him to run, as fear is a very powerful emotion and the fear of being maimed, being hurt or failing was greater then than the fear of not being accepted as a man.

But what is so relevant of that happening to the lives that follow? As we always point out on this particular subject, the same opportunity, the same chances to prove yourself will appear, the same kind of testing conditions surface, and that moment of confrontation between man and beast will re-appear in many forms until you have conquered, overcome and mastered those emotions that hinder your progress on this earth. It will always be so.

Then why do people study and delve into the field of re–incarnation? Some will do it out of sensationalism to prove how brave or great they were in a past life, especially if the present one was unsatisfactory, to give them confidence, to inflate their ego and also to prove to themselves that they could be someone respectable or great if they wished it to be. This you can be, but no matter what life condition you have chosen, the situations and happenings you have run before in a previous reincarnation will re-occur, until you overcome them. Until you learn to conquer those lower emotions, you will be confronted with a certain event which will recur again and again. What we are trying to illustrate to you is that reincarnation is a natural science which can aid you on your spiritual path, it can aid you in your material life and can help you to refine those emotions that are yet of a very coarse substance. Every time you manage to conquer the lower emotions that are hindering you in your path of evolution, you will join that higher self of yours which needs no further improvement. That has already reached this perfect state. You might be reincarnated as a king and yet, as a powerful ruler or monarch, you will be confronted with the same conditions as if you reincarnated as a beggar. Whatever you do with your material status, that is entirely up to you.

As you look at your life's chart, as you assess what is yet to learn and what has already been overcome, you will seek conditions and a life that will help you and give you the most opportunity to learn and to obliterate those deficiencies that are still in your spiritual make-up. For what a human spirit does not always remember is the fact that the higher self has already perfected the coarser emotions and is there available for you to draw from; in other words, if you have been a great pianist in a past incarnation, there is nothing to stop you drawing from that experience from your higher self. If you had been a master of many languages and a scholar, that academic knowledge is available to you because everything that you acquire is there for you to draw from. Many times you get credited with all sorts of ideas and we smile, for when you say thank you to us, you are saying thank you to your higher self, which is good, because any moment of humbleness and going inwards is a moment when you communicate with your higher self. Very often you draw strength and knowledge from your higher self and you just do not know it, and you can draw from it much more in the future now you have been made aware of it.

The wisdom of the ancient is there for all and each new life will bring a new sorting out and a new awareness, so that the life of an atheist or agnostic is not that which happens by accident. The soul which chose that particular life to shut out the Creator from all of their thinking is very often in a particular difficulty, as for the human spirit to shut out the source of life, the light and the love, is like living in a dark prison. Instead of deriding those that have chosen to live without the light and the love we can give compassion, for there is a dark world within us all where all the experiences we have are recorded, and it is your higher self which rejoices with you when you have conquered another fear, another emotion. Greatness is only great when it encloses the love and the light of God and appreciation of the brotherhood of man and the fatherhood of God. When you utter the words and desires not to reincarnate again in the earth plane, it can be so, for there are many planets in this universe where you can exist in various different forms and shapes which will all aid you in your path of evolution, for life in this universe is variable. There are so many shapes, some of them would horrify you and yet others would fill you with awe and inspiration, as you would like to be like them, but they live on finer mental vibrations than people on this earth do.

The only thing which is impossible is to regress into animal form, because there is always progression where nature is concerned. The only time nature regresses is when man-made interference occurs and that is not so much a regression, but more a form of temporary distraction, yet out of distraction will re-emerge a creation, something new. There is never an end, there is always change. There is always birth and rebirth for that is the natural law, and as the dying process is a birthing process – a birth into a different dimension, but a rebirth into a new world – there is no death.

The natural science of reincarnation is absolute. There is no beginning. There is no end. All the beauty that is within and without leaves its imprint on the spirit and the consolation to the spirit is the fact that the spirit is indestructible and that all the horror and the negative aspects, all experiences, can be wiped out. They are all catalysts for a new beautiful creation, new beginnings, new emergence to a higher and better existence. There is no end, there is only beginning in all. The pathway you have called your life is a chapter, a very small one on the path of your evolution which will enable you to reach the heights that your spirit hungers for.

HEALING

We cannot hope to build a better world without improving
the individual. Towards the end, each of us must work
towards his own highest development, accepting . . . . his
share of responsibility in the general life of humanity.
Marie Curie

I am permitted to be part of these communications and I am very pleased to be able to do so. I am a doctor. I was going to say, "I was a doctor." No, I still am a doctor because the very essence of me is that of a doctor. I liked nothing better than to help somebody recover from an illness and to me, the medical profession was just pure enjoyment. It was not a necessity that I felt I had to do, but was something I wanted to do with every fibre of my whole existence. Since that is the essence of me, my spirit, my former self, I still regard it as a privilege to aid humanity and the healing of the human psyche because, as many people are now aware, all ill health arises from disharmony in the human psyche.

What is healing? Healing is the most noble form of service when the healer, whether he is in the medical profession, a layman, a charismatic healer or an instrument for spiritual healing, aids another being in the recovery of his physical body and this service is of the highest and the best. There are great healers in your environment. Some work quietly, unobtrusively and humbly and with no credit for their services, the knowledge of having been of help or of service to their fellowmen or fellow creatures being sufficient. The student of metaphysics and of mysticism is often confronted with certain ideologies and philosophies and the question arises, is it dangerous to heal, or is it interference with the natural law? Isn't that person meant to suffer a particular physical ailment in order to learn a lesson? Well, if we adhere to the basic philosophy of cause and effect and apply that, yes, we do interfere, but we must not forget the law of compassion, that by helping the human spirit to evolve a little quicker, bringing it nearer to its own path of spiritual fulfilment we bring this being nearer to its spiritual goal.

The spiritual healing is where the healer is learning to tune into a spiritual energy which will then pass through the healer to the person the healer is trying to help. The energy comes from spirit, through spirit, to spirit, is of spiritual origin, comes from the spiritual source and is a very strong source of healing as it is diluted and each recipient absorbs as much as he or she can absorb at that moment of time. The quality of the channel who channels the spiritual energy plays an important role in that type of healing. Spiritual healing energy is very strong. The full force of it would shatter the physical body into little atoms and could not be contained into the physical body, which is why it has to be toned down. There are people like myself who, in different lives, have always been interested in healing, first through the curative powers of the herbs and the pendulum, then later as a doctor of orthodox medicine where I managed to make a name for myself and achieve a certain fame.

At this stage, I would like to introduce myself. I was Dr. Robert Koch, of German origin, and our writer here will be familiar with the fact that I was instrumental in the discovery of the tubercle bacillus. This does not come as a surprise to this channel for she herself succumbed to the disease in her last lifetime. Sometimes, to my great shame, I was pleased by my success, but there was always a driving ambition to find a cure for this terrible disease, which was also called consumption as the physical body was consumed by this virulent tubercle bacillus. It is quite natural to me that I would continue to aid and help humanity in the healing of human ills.

We talked about this spiritual energy and how it had to be diluted because spiritual energy is very powerful. There is a learning process involved to channel it correctly and dedication is needed so the healer can tune in and pass it on to the person who is being helped. This, as we have pointed out, is from spirit, through spirit, to spirit and each spirit will absorb as much as he or she can absorb at that particular time. First we start healing the spirit, (the psyche). It will be a cleansing process and as soon as the healing is taking effect within the spirit, it will affect the physical and the healing process has started. Even in cases of incurable or fatal physical diseases where there appears to be no apparent improvement, there is still a healing progress going on. Even though it might not be evident to the physical eye or to the physical being who receives it, the spirit is being healed, and in that case, is being prepared for a return journey to its spiritual home and being made fit to travel. So, it is never, ever wasted.

In the case of absent spirit healing where you give from your mind healing to another mind, what you are actually doing with your mind is that you are tuning in through your meditation and prayers. These are received because on your thought waves, the thought waves from the spirit are then directed on to the recipient and very good results are obtained by this as well. It often helps if there can be a kind of physical contact established at first which then acts like a magnet and the healer can tune in more completely, to continue the process of healing via the mind. All this is of spiritual origin and goes entirely from mind to mind, yet still from spirit, through spirit, to spirit and thus the spiritual energy is channelled correctly.

In the form of spiritual healing, the channeller of spiritual healing is not drained, as part of the spiritual energy that flows through them, not only revitalises the recipient, but also the channeller. However, if the channeller is not in top physical shape and still channels healing, the healing is still effective to a certain extent, but not to the degree it would be if there was good physical health. In this case it is even more diluted. Some of the spiritual energy stays within the healer so he can still feel better than before the act of healing, but as the spiritual energy has been diluted, the recipient is actually losing out. It is advisable that the healer either has a resting period or receives spiritual energy via another and fitter healer, resting until he or she is in better condition. That is why it is advisable when there is sickness within the healer, to avoid being a channeller of spiritual energy.

You may have heard of another form of healing, known as magnetic healing, and we would like to point out the difference. Many people are born with a certain ectoplasmic magnetic psychic energy and these people are able to pass on this strong magnetic psychic energy to another person. They pass it out from their body from the region of the solar plexus and you find these people often have a very strong and firm abdomen and stomach. They pass on this energy to the recipient, but after having done so they are normally in a state of depletion because with this magnetic psychic energy some of their own life force is mingled and instead of feeling replenished and refreshed, a state of exhaustion sets in. Their blood sugar level is low, their energy is low and they can be in a very negative physical state. They *have* obtained results and they always will obtain results in healing, but in that case there are no higher intelligencies at work who can discern and really know how much a spirit in the physical body can take. The magnetic charismatic healer who channels his energy through the solar plexus can, with that energy, remove pain and can cover up a physical deficiency which will then induce into the recipient a feeling of well being, but the ailment or the disease has not been cured. It will be dormant and the magnetic psychic energy acts like an analgesic, a pain killer. Once that has worn off and the energy has been used up by the recipient, in many cases it could then be too late as, for example, a ruptured appendix or peritonitis which could have been cured by operation and the correct post-operative treatment, in which case the person would have a premature death.

That is the difference between the healer and channeller of spiritual healing energy and that of the possessor of magnetic psychic healing energy. The latter is a substance which accumulates in the body. In some cases the psychic magnetic healer can in a way tune in and draw into his body a psychic energy, but if they refuse to listen or adhere to any natural law of spiritual intelligence, they can then interfere, intervene, with catastrophic results, It is not our intention to judge and decry another man's vocation. All we are trying to do is point out the difference between the two healing facilities.

Contrary to the modern way of thinking, the spiritual healer does not need any medical knowledge whatsoever. The spiritual healer is an instrument for the spiritual healing energy and channels it with sincerity and the desire to be of help to his fellow beings. Whether they are of animal form or humans, that does not matter for where there is life there is spirit and spiritual energy. So there is no need to have a medical degree and, contrary to modern belief, many doctors of medicine are inspired, helped and guided by spiritual intelligences and besides being good men of medicine, they are good healers. It should be the spiritual healer's duty always to seek medical advice when there is any sign of a serious physical or medical disorder, then in conjunction with the spiritual energy, the healing process can begin.

Like so many good inventions, the majority of curative medicine is inspired where the researcher has learned in his serious endeavour to tune into the etheric world, to obtain information and help in order to invent a new medicine which will abolish or cure a particular nasty disease and so far help his fellowmen, but as we have said, sometimes, like all good things, instead of being used correctly they will get abused. Because of material and physical stress, many good medical practitioners have forgotten how to listen, how to use their instinctive senses and the importance of a quiet assured presence and knowledge of the medical mind in a reassuring manner with a cheerful and loving countenance. They have forgotten how to use it and it has become so much easier to prescribe a curative medicine of a chemical substance which will either over stimulate the body, or the patient then abuses their physical body by taking too many chemical substances. As in all things, it should be done with common sense, the ideal way being that research should be intensified because there is a cure for every human ailment available if man could only make time to find out.

As the physician is trying to put a physical disorder back in good working order, the channeller of spiritual energy will start the healing process with the spirit so that there is harmony once again between body and spirit and the disease can be wiped out. Again, it is entirely up to the individual. To me it appears logical and to have far more sense to make oneself available as a channel for spiritual energy, to have a mind-to-mind, spirit-to-spirit contact and let the higher intelligences decide how much the recipient can take in order to live within the natural law of that energy. That alone brings harmony to any spirit.

You have learned that the true channeller of spiritual energy is replenished at the end of the healing session. The possessor of the magnetic psychic healing gift is depleted and a certain time has to elapse before they can replenish their energy. You decide the time needed for your gift, but once you have learned how to tune in correctly through these higher intelligences you will learn when the time has been sufficient, so you will abstain from giving further healing until a certain time span has elapsed and your physical body is replenished. In that way you will never be drained, depleted or exhausted but instead you are a true channel for the spiritual energy.

The more compassion and the more love for all life there is in the channeller, the more effective the spiritual energy will be. Remember, even though there might be no visible sign of a physical cure, the spirit will have received healing. Neither is there any discernment or judgment on the part of the spiritual intelligences whether the sufferer deserves or has a right to receive healing because the spiritual intelligencies know that spiritually everyone has an equal chance. Many times the physician in your hospitals has to decide whether it would be worthwhile to prolong the life of someone or whether all that has been done is enough. The spiritual intelligences make no such decision, for their philosophy is the philosophy of reality, this reality being that there is no death, only life, so they don't face that dilemma. To them, death is a change of progress into a different, lighter dimension and it is not just the shattering of a personality and the fragment that survives, the whole personality survives that experience you call death.

I am part of that experience. I am proof of that experience. Perhaps my time will come where once again I will walk amongst you to be given the privilege and the chance to heal. I myself will listen to the advice of superior intelligences and to the inspiration and love of God, and I will know whether it will be right to do so. It is up to you which way you want to go. Remember, from our point of view you are as good as your fellowman. You have a right to life, eternal life. That is the reality, the spirituality of all that is life.

May God guard you, guide you and inspire you, all the time.

HEALING II

*In order to terminate all suffering, be earnest in per-
forming good deeds. Let us unite in the practice of what
is good, cherishing a gentle and sympathising heart, carefully cultivating good faith and righteousness.*

Buddha

It is such a noble thing to be instrumental in channelling healing and
to alleviate suffering, but it is a very controversial subject, accepted
by many, rejected by a lot, even totally ridiculed at times, and many
times it is abused or misused like all things that come from God. So
it is always very joyful and uplifting to hear where there has been a
total cure and the person has once again been made whole.
Naturally, this makes the headlines in your media and the people
who were instrumental in that healing are then hailed as Messiahs or
great healers. However, in many cases from a physical and material
point of view we have to admit to defeat, but we have to point out
again the fact that each soul, each spirit, comes back to work out his
or her Karma, choosing a particular life or environment which
enables them to do so.

Many people choose an incarnation of very humble and poor
origin from a material point of view, in order to learn the lesson of
striving and overcoming all the obstacles and rise to great heights so
they can obtain material wealth. There are souls who are proud of
their humble origins and will never forget those who are still
struggling and striving, helping them whenever they can. Yet there
are others who, in their striving, forget the less fortunate ones and
can only think of their own need, their own desires in order to obtain
power or wealth and they manipulate others. Each according to their
choice. Remember the reason we point this out is that people chose
themselves.

When you have a case where the healer (and we now talk about
the spiritual healer) channels the spiritual energy through his or her
body to the patient and manages to cure them, there is great

rejoicing and in many cases the people are so touched by it that they are spiritually awakened and dedicate their life by serving God in helping others.

There are others who, when cured, soon forget and carry on with their selfish, self-absorbent lives searching for material wealth and power.

What about those who are humble souls, kind, loving and caring, yet they suffer a lot of illnesses and diseases, in great physical pain and in some cases mental anguish. What about those? Because they are very good souls, people wonder why these good souls have to suffer so much and they ask the question, "Is there a God who allows it?" God is the giver of all life, of all love, of all spiritual love. He gives people a chance to work off some of their Karma which they have accumulated in many lifetimes. Those good souls are given healing and no cure is achieved, yet through the channelling of the spiritual healing energy their spirit receives healing and strength to bring them great inner peace for them to be able to bear their pain with fortitude. The healing in that case is not a failure. The whole exercise of channelling spiritual healing energy is never a failure because a result has been obtained which is not visible to the physical eye, to the physical observer. In some cases the spirit then passes over to go back to his home in the spiritual world and there it has new life, new strength, all of a spiritual nature. The physical body which was a vehicle and was given a chance to learn, is disregarded as you would throw off a coat which kept you warm for many years and you were grateful for its warmth, but which you do not need any more once you embark on your journey home.

When we mourn should we really mourn an overcoat? No, we should give thanks that we were in the presence of that life, because by its example we learn lessons for, through the physical body, that soul expressed love, service and strength and touched other lives, enabling them to learn lessons. That is what we gather for, to give thanks for that life, to wish it well and Godspeed on its journey, and we shed a tear or two for times gone by when memories invade our minds. Quite rightly so, for saying goodbye and coping with bereavement is part of the lessons we learn. As we learn to cope with the arrival of a new life in this world, it is quite natural we should learn to cope with a departure.

What about those who appear to reject all healing that affects their spiritual or material being? In such a case, that spirit has decided long ago not to accept it, but to suffer regardless. That is their choice and it gives other souls a chance, with their service to that soul, to work off part of their Karma. So, again, there is no waste. Again, the channelling of the spiritual healing energy has not been a wasted exercise, for once that soul who appears cannot be helped, accepts the condition, they too find a strength to carry on.

At a particular time, a thought might enter the head to end their life, to terminate it themselves, because the thought of painful suffering and watching loved ones' faces as they observe the suffering is too much to bear. Is it right to end a physical life because of this? Whether it is right or wrong, again is the choice of the individual. Each spirit will realise after their departure from this world when a stocktaking takes place – which, by the way, they do themselves – that their new found spiritual vision helps them to see which was harmful and which was good for their spiritual evolvement. They then realise what was right and what was wrong. As for the man-made law which was passed down through your religion, "thou shalt not kill", physical destruction and forceful ending of a physical life is against the natural law because each life should run its natural course. That is part of the natural law and the spirit who lives within the natural law is aware of that, but again there are circumstances where the law of compassion operates, the law of compassion which alleviates pain and suffering. This law is all love and that law brings healing. So no prayer on behalf of another man, another fellow spirit is wasted. All prayers for the benefit and well being of a fellow man is a donation, a donation which will be taken and will be a brick to build a peaceful and spiritually more contented world.

Just as you put your monetary offerings into boxes provided by your churches so that the churches can be preserved for worship and shelter, your prayers are the bricks to build a better and a brighter world. So are your actions and your deeds, and the healer who dedicates his or her life to the service of channelling healing is part of that master plan.

All those who walk in the light, and there are many who heal who are humble souls not easily recognised at times, are servants of God who, regardless of ridicule, regardless of poverty or lack of funds, serve by channelling healing energy. Whether it is from mind to mind or their body has been made available for channelling spiritual healing, they carry on and there will be many more. They do it with humility with their hearts and minds filled with compassion for all sick creatures of this world.

As we said earlier, medical knowledge is not a necessary qualification to channel spiritual healing energy. A selfless, truthful, positive outlook on life, a sincere desire to serve is sufficient. There are rules to be observed, just as your doctors of orthodox medicine have to observe ethical rules. It is always wise to have a male and a female attending to a patient because we have to allow for the quirks in people's characters and not all people's thought processes are as pure or as positive. Many are invaded with demonic thoughts or negative thinking and they wish or have decided to misread the helpful gestures of their fellowmen, so it is very wise indeed to follow the ethical rules, to leave the diagnosis to the doctors of medicine and let God do the rest, knowing all will be well.

What man forgets, no matter what service or what form or shape of healing you have decided to do, whether it is by orthodox medicine, via herbalism, acupuncture or many others, let God be part of it. Let your instinct be guided by Him for He knows what is right for us – we forget. We are often overshadowed by material worry and we are also constantly bombarded with the force of modern advertising when the headlines scream at us what to do and what not to do, yet if we only would let ourselves be guided by this God instinct that is within all of us, all would be well.

So keep your body clean, dress it in natural fibre which will cut out the static electricity that man-made fibres can cause. Eat healthy food to keep your body in good shape and your thoughts on a positive level.

Reach out with your mind to that source, let God do the rest and all will be well. That is how simple healing is. Use it correctly, try not to abuse it – it is God's gift and remember when you feel that you have not achieved anything, it has not been wasted. Not an ounce of spiritual energy which is channelled is ever wasted. It will always achieve the result that is necessary for that particular moment, for God knows. If we accept that with humility then we have gone a step further ahead on the path of spiritual evolution.

CHAPTER 12

MUSIC AND COLOUR IN HEALING

For sweet is music and sootheth the soul and, like a heavenly chorus, awakes a thousand singing voices in the heart.

Proust

In continuing the subject of healing, we would like to point out how music and colour can help you, enhance and stimulate your life, making it far more beautiful than it is. It is part of the simplicity of life which many people forget or put aside. Overshadowed by materialism they are so busy going from place to place, looking fearfully over their shoulders for whatever will happen next, and in all that haste forgetting the calming effect of the delicate hues of all colours or how soothing the sounds of music can be. You are reminded of it in the writings of the great poets and philosophers, how music soothes the savage beast, how it can sometimes ease or eradicate pain and bring light to banish the darkness surrounding you.

Scientists are working in their laboratories looking for cures for new threatening diseases, the sicknesses of your times that are really the effects of the abandonment of principles and moral ethics. What we are trying to do is to remind you of the very simple remedies which will give you a feeling of well being, a renewed strength and a source to recharge your batteries regardless of your creed. Where God is concerned, there is no creed. No-one is singled out, for as far as He is concerned you are all the chosen ones, His beloved children. He looks upon you with love and fondness and yet He lets you grow in the way you choose. We are with you, surrounding you at all times in days of darkness and nights of sleeplessness, when you are going through difficult periods and are looking for the light. We are there to encourage you, hoping to ease your burden with the love of our Father which unites us in a bond because we are all from the same family, we have the same roots and that invisible thread, the spark that unites us, binds us together, for we all strive for the same goal. We are with you in your striving, by your side to point out remedies you can take to soothe you and take away the pain.

You hear through your radio and all the other instruments which produce your music that love changes everything. It does change everything, it is only the cynics who say that love isn't all. It is, everything. Without it you are nothing and it does not matter how few material things you possess, if you have love, you are richer than a millionaire.

There is no specific rule about what type of music you should listen to. Listen to the music that appeals to you, which soothes and quietens you and dispels any darkness surrounding you. The music that brings back light to your life and brightens it will relax you, helping you to think straight and positively once again. Those of you who have the clairvoyant sight to see the colours that music can produce, will realise what healing benefit listening to music can bring. The type of music you choose is entirely up to you. If it appeals to you, the harp is indeed a wonderful instrument which has always been associated with a heavenly or spiritual aspect, so the soft notes of the harp would be a soothing and healing remedy for a shattered nervous system, to dispel all the greyness you have accumulated during a busy day. If you want to be lulled into passive mental state, the gentle lilting sound of the pipes of Pan will give you a tranquil state of mind. If you are longing to dream, to relax and let the cares of the day be washed away, then listen to a mixture of violins and piano, but do try, if you can, to avoid the harsh beating of drums and all the new synthetic sounds which are so prevalent today.

Your spirit is delicate and hungry for peace and it needs a gentle soothing sound to quieten it, so be kind to your spirit at the end of a hard day. When you listen to the soft, lilting sounds of the harp you can be transported back to the Elysian Fields, bringing back memories to your spirit of times gone by where there was no materialism, where only beauty and light were your constant companions; times when the fragrance and beauty of a single flower gave you intense pleasure, the intricate colour system of the wings of a butterfly enchanted you and the sounds of laughter and children playing brought you joy and upliftment. These are the memories your spirit recalls before it was encased in a physical body and was free of any earthly desire for material goods. The sound of soft music will help you to remember and will soothe your spirit, renew your strength and your determination not to lose sight of your dreams and your goals.

When you listen to the music you have chosen which you feel will achieve this, then start to visualise the colours that this music brings. You should try to imagine a kaleidoscope of colours that are not of your world; blues so pale like the finest gossamer silk, white with a brilliance which none of your chemical detergents can achieve, lemon brighter than the sun itself and gold – the gold that is taken from the cosmic ray of the Christ spirit, the finest and the best which dominates all. It is that ray which is focused now on your earth plane bringing about a new awakening, a new upsurge of spiritual awareness and with it, reminders of simple remedies for the spirit of mankind, that spirit which has been in darkness now for many centuries whilst inhabiting the physical body.

Your spirit should be dominant, for the physical is just a moment that is gone. What you said, what you thought five minutes ago is past history, but what you are now and what you are going to be, that is eternal. It is important to let your spirit be the master and to remember that the master is waiting for the student to be ready. Your spirit has within it infinite wisdom and when you listen to the sweet sound of music and visualise all the beautiful pale colours that the music brings, you will feel refreshed and replenished. The most wonderful aspect of this is that you can take others with you on this journey of rediscovery by these simple remedies for healing and strengthening the spirit.

So be the master of your ship. Don't be like the leaf that is pushed and blown about by the autumn wind, but be guided by your spirit. Be absorbed by the beautiful colours and the sounds of music and if you will let yourself be guided by your spiritual instinct, you will find the path you have chosen is the right one.

Let the sound of music be the one that sends you to sleep and let the sounds of soft music awaken you. When you are weary and your strength is flagging, when tears are closer than the sounds of laughter, then let music soothe the savage beast.

CHAPTER 13

NATURE SPIRITS

Everything is fruit to me which thy seasons bring. O nature: from thee are all things, in thee are all things, to thee all things return.

Marcus Aurelius

Everything is part of a plan and everything has its place in God's creation, not one thing has been forgotten. Where there is life and the breath of life of God there is a form of protection, a guardian or a spirit who will be the spiritual protector and guide of that particular life. Look at the perfect construction of a tree, lean against it, press your life form to that of the tree and you will feel the life pulsating. You can sense the life force of the tree running into your body and a feeling of peace and serenity will overcome you. Every tree, every plant has nature spirits who are their protectors. They have taken on the colour of the tree and are shaped like miniature humans, but they are entities who have never incarnated in the physical form. They are content to take care of plants that are put into their trust.

As you walk through your forests today you will become aware of trees where there is an absence of life force, being devoid of all life and this is a result of man's wrong-doing by use of chemicals. In that case nature spirits had to leave the trees and go deeper into the forests where man has not yet penetrated and abused the natural world. The chemicals used on your plants, flowers and trees drive away the spirit guardians as their use is not compatible with their existence and totally against the natural law. Ideally, anyone who possesses a garden should set aside a corner and leave it totally unspoiled, untouched by chemicals, and let all plants grow as nature intended. That little corner could be a haven which will also attract the nature spirits to them and no matter what plants you have decided to let grow in that wild, unruly corner they will be strong, beautiful, bright and pulsating with life. It would also be ideal if you could set aside a corner to grow herbs which would help to cure the ills besetting mankind and the herbs will also attract a nature spirit who will take care of them.

Those plants will not only be charged with the goodness and the curative qualities they possess, they will have an extra added ingredient, spiritual love, given to them by their nature spirit. So all that you can grow organically and without any man-made substance will thrive and be of a better quality, giving you a richer and better nourishment than any other plant.

Every flower has its own nature spirit and each takes on the shape and the colour of the flower itself. When you wander into your garden and if you have been spiritually awakened through meditation or participation in other spiritual activity, you will become aware of those beings and you will feel their love. They will return to you what you have given to their beloved plant, the beauty and the fragrance which will gladden your heart after a hard day's labour and brighten your existence. If your vision has expanded, if you possess patience and are filled with love for all nature, you will become aware of these creatures. Then you will see that the gossamer wings they possess take on the colour and the hues of the flowers. The sweet pea fairy with its utterly benign expression of love, joy and beauty will enchant you and you will be aware of the gratitude in its face as you give your love and care to the flowers.

Step out on a bright clear Spring morning, walk among your daffodils, bend your head, look intently into the trumpet of the daffodil and behold its beauty as you do so. You will feel the warmth and love of the daffodil spirit.

When man treats all things that grow with love and respect and when only the natural things that are available to him go into the earth, then the harvest will be bountiful because he will then reap beyond his expectations as the colours will be more enhanced, the greens will be brighter than ever before and the life force emanating from those flowers will have a healing benefit to all those who are in need. The flowers you take into your hospitals or to people who are sick, which have been grown with love and natural nourishment, will cheer and brighten the existence of the sick person.

Walk amongst the trees when you are weary. Lean against a chestnut and your frayed nerves will be calmed and soothed, for the chestnuts have a wonderful healing quality for your nervous system.

As you look up into the rich foliage of the chestnut tree, you will feel the life that is there. There will be no feeling of threat, only love. Walk to the oak, lean against it when you are tired, weary and exhausted and you will find after a while that strength will return to your tired limbs, for the nature spirits with their love for their charge will encourage the tree to pulsate the life and channel it to the weary human being leaning against it. But threaten that same tree, kick it or put your penknife into it to carve some initial and you might as well put that knife into another human. You may then feel threatened, nervous or apprehensive, for what harm has that tree done to you? It is only there to enhance a beautiful world and its guardian spirit will feel rejected, outraged and confused at being a witness to such thoughtlessness, as you would if someone threatened a loved one of yours.

These things are all part of life which pulsates for them as it does for you. If you live within the natural law you will show respect for all life because the person who accepts that everything has its place, everything is perfectly worked out, will accept that just as each living person has a guardian spirit watching over them as a conscience, inspiration, teacher and guide in times of need, each plant that has a life force has someone watching over it.

There is much desolation and despair amongst the natural world. Much life force has been withdrawn from areas that were once places of beauty and enhancement which are devoid of all life now, of all joy. They are indeed dead to your world, but a new awakening in man's consciousness is bringing about an awareness that all life is part of this universe and should be revered and respected. Every time you look at the perfect creation of a rose, inhale the delicate scent and feast your eyes on the glorious colour of that beautiful plant, fairies or nature spirits will have helped in that creation, for they too are on a path of service, to serve their Creator just like you.

Think before you get out your can of pesticides for you drive away beings whose only aim is to enhance your life and all life. There are other means of dispersing things which harm the plant. Man must learn to go back to the basics and simplicity of life and acknowledge the fact that all life is entitled to live. God in His wisdom has given everything that lives a guardian, a guide and in His perception all that life is equally dear to him, as it should be to you.

May the beauty of the universe have a deeper meaning to you from now on and may the scent of the roses awaken the desire in you to be a true observer of the natural law, the strength of the trees bring you healing and peace and may the light of God shine upon your path.

CHAPTER 14

THE MASTERS

There is . . . . in the minds of men, a certain presage of a
future existence! And this . . . . is most discoverable in the
greatest geniuses and most exalted souls.

Cicero

Many questions are asked about the Masters. Who are they? Where do they come from? What is their mission? Is it really true they are walking amongst us, visible yet not recognised, or are they part of mysteries and legends? No, they are part of the reality, they do exist. Yes, they do walk amongst us, unrecognised, There are others who claim, "I am an avatar," "I am a Master," "I have come here to do great works." Listen to them, for they too have something to say and you can learn from them all, as you can learn from all things.

The Masters are those who have attained the ability to control the natural law that works for them, they are not victims of it. They know how to manipulate it, in other words they are the ones who can make objects appear and disappear, can turn water into wine and feed the five thousand with very little. They have attained and mastered the natural law and, if they wish, could remain in a permanent blissful state, but instead they have chosen to serve mankind, to watch over all the worlds, inspiring and helping all souls who struggle as they strive towards their spiritual goal. You might meet them or might have met them and not recognised them for they are able to appear in the physical at any time they wish. They never draw attention to themselves and deliberately assume a very ordinary countenance. When you are in their presence you feel that nothing is hidden from then. Have you not met someone like that where you feel the moment you are with them you are calmed and everything you feel and experience seems to be known, the pain you suffered subsides and problem that seemed unsurmountable can now be solved? That is what they can do, just by being very ordinary. You will not hear them boast about their knowledge or the wisdom they acquired, neither will they stagger you with their brilliant clairvoyance nor will they achieve a miraculous instantaneous cure of your ills, because the change within you will be a gradual and slow progress. They will be a catalyst, that after having been in their presence you will perceive the world and its inhabitants in a different light. You will retrace your footsteps and you will learn to think on a more spiritual and higher level by starting to think of the well being of your fellowmen first. Without realising it, you will have started on the pathway of service to God, in other words towards your brothers and sisters.

They very often mingle with the crowds when all you can perceive is a seething of humanity. At times they will be an invisible visitor and take part in your gatherings, be a teacher in your circle or your study group, a guest at your table or an inspiration in your moments of despair. You will be totally unaware of their presence. They give whether you think you deserve it or not. They will be there whether you call them or not for they will be drawn to you by the hidden desire to live a better, lighter life, more filled with love and hope. They will be instrumental in gently persuading you to change your ways of thinking and action.

So what do they do when they appear in the physical? Your local refuse collector who will smile at you, cheerfully collecting the debris of your daily life could be a Master. Another could be a dispenser of tea and sympathy or the person who holds the door open for you as you struggle, laden with shopping and who smiles and blesses you, or just a voice in your darkness that encourages you to keep on keeping on.

Where do they live, these masters? At places on your planet, never heard of, never dreamed of, where there is purity of thought and people live in harmony within the natural law; where there is no decay or darkness, a place where there is solitude and silence yet a silence filled with companionship and love, where even in the darkest night the stars shine brightly. There in the coolness of the desert night they gather in prayer and meditation to change the course of this destructive world, high up between the mountains of the Himalayas where the ancient wisdom is practiced and lived, from where they then go forth amongst the people of this world to dispense that wisdom, love and compassion. They rejoice when a soul who has been overcome and overshadowed by material worry has retraced its footsteps to walk on the path of faith and light and is trying to help others too. They try to bring harmony where there is an imbalance. They walk with your men of medicine to inspire them to cure the ills of mankind. They work closely in your orthodox churches where brilliant minds which could be bringers of spiritual wisdom are weighed down by dogmatic thought, trying to enlighten them and broaden their spiritual horizons, bringing them the wisdom of tolerance, understanding and compassion.

You have met them. You have met the doctors you would not glance twice at in the street. Perhaps the clothes are a little less neat and new, perhaps even a little shabby, he may have a limp, a twitch or lost his hair and have a weary expression. Gaze into the eyes, see the light and the compassion. Call him out in the darkest, wettest, coldest night and he will be there, or go to your spiritual caretaker, vicar or priest, no matter what time, only to be greeted with love and welcome, a welcome you can feel to be genuine. He may be riddled with arthritis and rheumatism in a draughty vicarage, yet his love is endless, has no boundary, no dogma attached to it. That is how you might meet them. Go into your slums where people are homeless, destitute, and you will find a caring man or women who will walk among them giving food and drink, blankets and comfort, showing no fear for you will not see them harmed as they cannot be harmed.

They are with you now, trying to help and show the way on this new wave of enlightenment, this New Age you have entered. You are part of the dawning of that New Age, you are in it and they stimulate the thoughts towards it, show all the venues available, are even instrumental in starting new philosophies, beliefs and pathways of spiritual rediscovery. Did not the Master Jesus say, "Pass you not a beggar in the street for you will be passing me." Give generously. His commandment, "Love one another," was His mission in His short span of earth life. It is still His mission now, not to be the source of a new religion, but to be an inspiration to all mankind in the simplicity of life, an instrument that brings forth the truth of the Christ Spirit, that enlightens all pathways whether you are Jews or Gentiles, orthodox or unorthodox, just to remind you of the fact that, "The Father and I are one". As He healed the sick, helped the lost to find their way again, feeding those with spiritual wisdom who were hungry for it and distributed food to many thousands, still having some left over, just remember, "Seek you first the Kingdom of Heaven and it shall be added on to you". He used the brother Francis when He joined the Masters and demonstrated His great compassion for all life, telling the world, "It is in giving that we receive."

Rejoice in the fact that the cosmic rays of the Christ Spirit are focused on your planet, Earth, fully for the first time and that those who have mastered the mysteries of life walk with you.

Remember those that are in need. Give generously of your love. Love one another.

May the Christ light overshadow you, strengthen you and lighten your life.

CHAPTER 15

LIFE

I sent my Soul through the Invisible,
Some letter of my After-life to spell:
And by my Soul return'd to me,
And answer'd 'I Myself am Heav'n and Hell'.
The Rubáiyát of Omar Khyyám

As we are entering the era of the New Age, people are beginning to realise that the breath of God is in all that lives, all that is animated, all that grows, and they are becoming aware of their environment. They are starting to question, what is it all about, why are we here; is it only to acquire material possessions, bigger and better houses, bigger bank balances, designer clothes and the latest model in cars or interior design? Many who have reached the pinnacle of their material success look around and find that it was not what they were looking for, there is something missing in their lives, still an emptiness which no money can buy. After having tasted all the material pleasures that are available to them, there is still this emptiness. Very often one can see these people portrayed in glossy magazines or on the televisions screens and can see that emptiness; their eyes seem to be dead, they are moving, they appear to be smiling, but the spark of life seems to be missing and to be asleep.

It is about this spark that we want to talk. How do we ignite it? Is it absolutely necessary to join a religious order to become spiritually aware? Is it essential for our spiritual well being to be on our knees, to pray constantly? Is it essential to abolish all material possessions, to live simply without any trappings or world contacts in order to obtain spiritual riches and contentment? As in all these things, we cannot generalise. For one person it might be essential to join one religious order or another for a special creed in order to have a certain spiritual discipline and spiritual exercise for them to adhere to. Another person will discover their spiritual self by observing nature, by being more aware of their natural environment and trying to observe a healthier, more natural life. Each spirit will find their own way and we are not here to judge another man's belief. It is not our duty to condemn any religious order, for every free spirit has a right to follow the path they choose, regardless of colour or culture. When we incarnate in a physical body, as our minds are tainted with special doctrines we are inclined to forget that wonderful gift we are given with the gift of life, the gift of free will. We are very often so easily influenced, so easily led, thinking that only by doing what others tell us to do can we find the spiritual contentment and freedom we are seeking.

It is only by the way we choose that we find spiritual contentment and harmony. That is the only way, regardless of what that way is. If we find inner peace, feeling that we are growing spiritually and mentally on the path we follow, then we know, we are aware, and we do not need anybody to point that out to us. We *know*, it is an inner realisation which comes to us that this path is right for us. As we are all children in the spiritual sense, regardless of physical age, we like to be left to our own devices at times. At other times we like to be told so that when we are out in the wilderness, when we have lost sight of our spiritual goal and the true meaning of our existence, we are only too eager to cry out for guidance, for a pointer which will show us the right direction. For each spirit a way will be shown according to that spirit's need, so when we pray and ask for guidance and spiritual riches to be given to us, they will be given according to our need. We shall always be given what we are ready to absorb. With our limited vision, as we are so used to judging everything according to the material, physical appearances, we are not always aware that what is given to us is sufficient. We feel we should have better, bigger or greater things, so we ignore spirit's true gifts in our frantic search.

Many times, voices, filled with anguish and despair cry out, "Please help me, God, please show me that way," and help is given, but those asking for help often don't recognise this fact because they are suffering from a spiritual lack of vision and spiritual deafness.

Now you will say, quite rightly, "how do we know which is the correct thing for us, how do we know we are not being misled?" Is it not the very fact that when you think you have been given help and follow it, things went right? Oh, ye of little faith. We have said, "Ask and it shall be given, knock and it shall be opened unto you." Of course you know what will give you peace, that which is of a spiritual pureness and simplicity which will calm your troubled spirit, heal and purify, not that which gives you turmoil, discontentment and restlessness. Things that are of true spiritual value and give you peace are for you alone. You can share this knowledge if you wish, yet always realising that what has been given to you in a particular way might not suit your brother or your sister, but you can tell them reassuringly that for them, too, there is a way; for them to listen and the answer will be spiritual peace and contentment. It will not be, as you might think, that you will then feel spiritually somnambulous or in a sleep-like state where you are quite content to sit back and do nothing. Spiritual peace is something that, when you find it, only you can define it. You will have harmony, you will feel and care for all that is life, but your emotions will be under control.

You will have realised by now that when you are ruled by your emotions you are unable to be of use to anyone. It is only by learning to control your emotions, to be master of them, that you can be of true service to God. That is your mission in life, to learn to control your emotions and, by mastering them, you will be master of your fate because you will be in absolute control.

As you start to become aware when you go on your spiritual quest in life, you realise that man does not live by bread alone and when your spirit needs food in order for you to function correctly and in harmony, so you open up. At first it is a revelation as you start on your quest. You realise then that you have been suffering from a spiritual mal-nutrition and you start to feed your spirit by reading, by attending seminars, going to retreats, going to houses of worship and generally you are like a soul that has been in the wilderness, in a desert, and is starved of spiritual companionship and spiritual food. In your material life, there is always a parallel spiritual condition. As a small child you learn – as your parents say – the "hard way", you eat food, sometimes too much in abundance or too quickly. The result is that you have gastric trouble and pains and you feel unwell and the spiritual parallel is that when you learn your spirit has been starved of food, you can suffer from over indulgence. You are in search of clarity and yet with the haphazard way you feed your spirit, instead of clarity a state of confusion sets in and many an ardent quest ends with a withdrawal from all spiritual activities because the confusion has not aided you in your quest. You feel it has not been worthwhile for, as your vision is extended with your new spiritual awareness, as you hear people talking in wise, quiet and peaceful tones of voice about the love of God, light and peace, then you see the same people committing acts of untruths, overshadowed by jealousy, in the possession of an oversized ego wanting to be reassured, worshiped and put on a pedestal, with your new found vision you do not find that compatible with the wisdom you have heard about. Disillusion sets in, but you have to stop and think.

You see, no spirit ever walks alone. The Master is willing and waiting when the student is ready. You, too, have your Master to guide you and give you encouragement on your pathway. It is not the people we judge who disillusion us with their erratic behaviour which we find so incompatible with our new found belief, it is we ourselves that are at fault. The first thing one learns in that awareness, is, "Judge not and be not judged." The acquirement of knowledge is easy! Through literature and the forms of your media, material is available in abundance and it is comparatively easy to utter words of wisdom and advice, but the understanding and total absorption of that wisdom – that is difficult. So we have to use our imagination yet again. Visualise all the academics in your world, all the knowledge and wisdom that they have accumulated which they teach to young enquiring minds. Do they understand, fully comprehend the wisdom of Plato, Socrates, Plutonius? Do they know the true meaning of that quotation which begins, "I sent my Soul through the Invisible?" Are they ready, do they understand that they alone are responsible for their life and how to live it?

Oh, what a beautiful dream – no war, no jealousy, no greed, no destructiveness, no killing in the name of God, universal love, Brotherhood of Man, Fatherhood of God, paradise revisited! Yes, it is a beautiful dream, but that is what you are searching for, the paradise you read about, this Shangri-la you have heard about where there are no visible signs of advancing age, where body and spirit are eternally young, where there is peace, love and harmony. "Oh, God, why has Thou forsaken me," you cry. This paradise exists. Stop looking now. Stop rushing into the next bookshop for writings of the great philosophers who were helpful in your search and do not read until you find the answer within yourself. Paradise is within you, in your mind, in your spirit. This Shangri-la exists, but you won't let it exist; in your constant search for spiritual fulfilment you shut it out and the images that appear are distorted.

You are too obsessed with what impression you make on your fellow man and the image that reflects in your looking glass is too critical; is the garment you are wearing still fashionable enough, are lines of ageing on your face disguised sufficiently so you can appear younger and fitter? Look again, look at the eyes that look back at you. Do you see joy? Do you see love? Do you understand that love or do you see pain and sadness? When you start to understand spiritual wisdom you see all these things for they are all you, and behind the sadness you see the paradise you lost, the infinite peace of eternal light, the eternal you that is forever young and forever loved.

Cling to that image when you look. Do not shut out that paradise of yours, for with realisation and understanding that you alone are the possessor of that paradise, the creator of your hopes and your will, that the power of your mind can make up images of light, of darkness, of great beauty yet of ugliness so great that you recoil, when you start to understand that knowledge, being aware of the responsibility which comes with it, you will never look back. You will give thanks for all the experiences that made you wise, healthy, spiritually wealthy and an instrument of love.

All the wisdom in the universe cannot help you if you do not understand this wisdom. Those of your fellow men who are just mouthpieces of spiritual utterances need your love as much as those who are aware and have understanding. Love is given freely to you so you can share it with all. The golden ray of the Master who walked the Earth overshadowed by that Christ spirit, is focused on this Earth once again. Visualise that ray, it will protect you against the negative images, against the forces of darkness. For the first time, the full power of that cosmic golden ray is focused on this planet, Earth, for unity is needed. There is great danger that the darker forces will turn towards destruction, so that ray is there to bring a balance.

If you want to walk with that ray and let the light of the Christos enlighten you it is your choice, for when that ray is focused on the planet, cures for diseases are invented, healing methods are discovered, Masters walk on footpaths unrecognised, yet very effective in their ministry and great man and women walk in that ray to be an inspiration to those that are in need of it.

Give love to those you call the less fortunate of your brothers, those who walk with the darker forces, touch them with your light.

All those who are not yet aware and have not yet understood the wisdom, the ancient wisdom, their time will come. Love them, place them in light. Seek and you shall find. Look within, for paradise is yours.

God be with you.

CHAPTER 16

PEARLS OF WISDOM

When you have reached this chapter you will have realised our aim is to bring you information, inspiration, love and light and if you have read so far we thank you for, as the Master Jesus said, "Some of the seeds will fall on stony ground," but that is irrelevant. You have eternity ahead of you. What you do not absorb now you will absorb at a future time when your spirit has been made fertile, ready to accept and receive the seed. Some of the seed will go into very fertile soil. It will feed a spirit that is hungry and ready to receive the spiritual food. There will be some that dismiss it who are not enlightened or who have chosen to walk a different path of service. May God bless them. There will be those who will question it and that is how it should be. Question, ask, seek. We welcome the hungry enquirer or seeker.

We are not here in your vicinity, near you, around you to condemn, as each and every person has the spiritual freedom to choose which way they wish to go. No matter which direction you choose, if you have love in your heart and do not try to force your belief onto another person, but are a being filled with love, giving generously of that love, then you are on the right way indeed, no matter what creed, colour, race or culture, for you are a child of God. You are doing the right thing by Him and it is of no consequence what you call your God as long as you are filled with love for all life.

Let the sands of time be your teacher, let the experience of life teach you how to love, to live and let all that happens to you be a valuable lesson. Take out of each experience the kernel of truth, letting that be the vitamins for your spirit to strengthen and fortify it. Be open-minded towards all things you cannot understand and if you try to give love to all those who deride and ridicule you, leaving them with a blessing, you are doing well. When the burden of your life weighs you down, remember God's love and the love He has given you is for eternity. The material and physical events are but a passing moment in that life of yours, but the light and goodness of all life lasts forever and the love you are seeking is within you. It is up to you to bring it forth and to nourish it.

Be kind to yourself. Forgive yourself. Try not to hanker after what has been, but live joyfully with what you have got. Take the goodness of your today's with you into the new brightness you have now found and you will accumulate riches beyond your dreams. Start each new day with a positive thought, "I walk with God, He is my shield. He is my light in my darkest hour. I will love and respect all life and I will have a good day," then you will indeed. Let no irritating behaviour deter you, for all that ails you has a cure in God's realm. Seek and you will find. Each brother and sister of your fellowmen you embrace with love, you embrace God. So let this love be your inspiration, let it be your guide and to those who disbelieve you or deride you, give them a blessing for their need is greater than yours.

Let these pearls you possess never lose their glow as the pearls, the jewels, you wear around your neck lose their glow when they are not against the life force of your skin. Cherish these pearls and they will glow. They will be the light and the glow in your darkest hour. They will strengthen you in your endeavours and remember, each and everyone of you, you are important, the Beloved. No matter who you are or what you do, do what you have chosen, do it with love and the irritations of everyday life will not bother you, for the love you feel for all things will outweigh all else. Remember you are as good as anyone, but not better because, regardless of all things, you are the pearls and you are part of this vast necklace we call life.

Peace be with you.